"Mistletoe," I said, working hard to keep my voice even. Had he really never seen it before? City folks were weird.

Mikah dropped the plant as if two of its tiny leaves had closed around his finger and bitten him. I didn't miss the small intake of breath or slight pink flush of his cheeks. The space between us suddenly felt like way too much and way too little at the same time. Never in my life had I experienced such an immediate, visceral attraction to someone. But it felt like more than a physical pull. It felt like connection. I wanted so much: wanted to pull him close, wanted to feel his soft curls as they slid between my fingers, wanted to trace the fine lines of his jaw. What I didn't want was to freak him out.

I cleared my throat. "Don't worry. Not gonna try to kiss you or anything."

Welcome to

Dreamspun Desires

Dear Reader,

Love is the dream. It dazzles us, makes us stronger, and brings us to our knees. Dreamspun Desires tell stories of love featuring your favorite heartwarming heroes, captivating plots, and exotic locations. Stories that make your breath catch and your imagination soar.

In the pages of these wonderful love stories, readers can escape to a world where love conquers all, the tenderness of a first kiss sweeps you away, and your heart pounds at the sight of the one you love.

When you put it all together, you find romance in its truest form.

Love always finds a way.

Elizabeth North

Executive Director
Dreamspinner Press

KD Fisher

A CHRISTMAS CABIN FOR TWO

PUBLISHED BY

DREAMSPINNER
PRESS

Published by
DREAMSPINNER PRESS

5032 Capital Circle SW, Suite 2, PMB# 279,
Tallahassee, FL 32305-7886 USA
www.dreamspinnerpress.com

This is a work of fiction. Names, characters, places, and incidents either
are the product of author imagination or are used fictitiously, and any
resemblance to actual persons, living or dead, business establishments,
events, or locales is entirely coincidental.

A Christmas Cabin for Two
© 2019 KD Fisher
Editorial Development by Sue Brown-Moore

Cover Art
© 2019 Alexandria Corza
http://www.seeingstatic.com/
Cover content is for illustrative purposes only and any person depicted
on the cover is a model.

Paperback ISBN: 978-1-64108-182-5
Digital ISBN: 978-1-64405-334-8
Library of Congress Control Number: 2019943703
Paperback published November 2019
v. 1.0

Printed in the United States of America
∞
This paper meets the requirements of
ANSI/NISO Z39.48-1992 (Permanence of Paper).

KD FISHER is a queer New England-based writer of authentic, heartfelt LGBTQ+ narratives. KD grew up all over the United States, bouncing from North Carolina to Hawai'i to Illinois, and finally settling in Maine where she spends far too much time at the beach.

When KD isn't writing, she can usually be found hiking with her overly enthusiastic dog, obsessing over plants, or cooking elaborate meals. She loves classic country, perfectly ripe tomatoes, and falling asleep in the sun.

Website: kdfisher.squarespace.com
Twitter: @kdfisher_author
Instagram: @kdfisherauthor

To Cooper, the best companion anyone could ask for.

Acknowledgments

FIRST, a million thank-yous to my wonderful family, chosen and blood. I love you all so much and am endlessly grateful for your support and encouragement. A special thank-you to Tara, who always reminds me to take joy in my work. And to Michael, my first and most attuned reader.

Thank you to my wonderful team of beta readers: Rebecca, SM, Quinn, Kat, and Daphne. Your advice and thoughtful feedback improved this story so much.

I'm so grateful to the entire team at Dreamspinner Press, especially Sue Brown-Moore, who supported this project from its inception.

And last but certainly not least, the biggest thank-you of all to my readers. I hope you enjoy reading Mikah and Matt's story as much as I enjoyed writing it!

Chapter One

Mikah

I DRAGGED a breath in through my nose and tried to catalogue the scents of my father's house: woodsmoke, furniture polish, espresso, citrus. The combination of smells was still too unfamiliar to be of any real comfort. My heart raced, and the next breath came in ragged. I stared into the fireplace. The flames chased crackling sparks, consuming the words hastily scrawled on notebook paper. Something inside me relaxed. I felt lighter. The letter was nothing but ash now. Gone forever.

"Mikah! *Che cosa fai?*" Elena's sharp voice snapped my gaze away from the fire. "What the hell are you doing?" she repeated in English, adding the expletive when I chose not to answer. "Please don't tell me you're sitting in here moping again." My sister tossed her perfectly tousled chestnut hair and thrust a sheet of paper into my hands.

"Want me to burn this too?" I asked, trying and failing to sound appropriately snarky.

"No, you idiot." She shook her head as her eyes flicked to the fireplace. "Naomi wants us to go pick up the Christmas tree."

I glanced down at the paper, an advertisement for some place called Haskell Farms boasting the opportunity to fell your own Christmas trees. Was my stepmother out of her mind? Really, I'd only met Naomi a handful of times before deciding to spend over a month in her home for the holidays, so I couldn't be sure. She had, after all, agreed to marry my father with all of his grandiose bluster and his tendency to spend every waking moment at the office.

"Um, Elena." I dragged the tip of my finger over the words on the flyer. "This says you can cut down your own tree. I don't think I've ever even *seen* a chainsaw in real life."

This comment earned me an extravagant sigh. "Ugh, can you at least try not to sound so pathetic? It'll be fine. Besides, Naomi's been running herself ragged getting everything ready for the golden boy's arrival. It's the least we can do." As irritating as my sister could be, I had to admit she was solicitous. From the moment her plane touched down at the Jackson Hole Airport, Elena had bustled around, cleaning, running errands in town, and generally being her exuberantly pleasant self. Conversely, I'd holed up in my impeccably decorated bedroom like a brooding thirteen-year-old since my arrival two days earlier.

"Why don't we just go to the grocery store like normal people? They sell trees, right? Plus isn't it kind of early for that? Jesus, El, Thanksgiving was *yesterday*. Can we at least have a few days devoid of holiday merriment?" I knew I was not about to win the argument.

"Overpriced. And no." Elena clucked. "Naomi said the one they got in town last year lost all its needles right away. Let's go. It'll be fun. And you need to get out of the house. Pretty please." She tugged on the sleeve of my hoodie. Her whining reminded me so much of my students, I had to school my features to hide the grimace of regret.

"Fine." I sighed and took one final glance at the fire.

I followed my sister into the large foyer, all rustic pine beams and gleaming hardwood floors, still unwilling to let go of my sullen silence. Elena chattered on about the drive and what kind of tree we should look for. We could get the mangiest of Charlie Brown Christmas trees for all I cared. Pulling on my totally impractical black combat boots and insufficiently warm denim jacket, I almost jumped when Naomi's manicured hand landed on my shoulder. Her enormous diamond ring glinted in the weak winter sun.

"Are you kids going to get the tree?" She looked thrilled, bright smile and soft eyes.

"Yup! Need us to get anything else while we're out?" Elena yanked up the zipper of her far more sensible black parka.

Naomi put her index finger to her lips in consideration before gesturing for me to hand her the flyer. "Right. I thought so. They have a farm stand too. If they have any Yukon Gold potatoes or something similar, get about two pounds. I was thinking of doing steaks tomorrow night since your dad said that's Luca's favorite. And, of course, feel free to pick up anything else you guys want."

"Got it!" Elena beamed as Naomi handed her some cash. I said nothing.

As we trudged across the snowy driveway, I cut my eyes at my sister. "I'm driving."

At first I was relieved. For once Elena wasn't going to argue or insist she knew how to drive and then subject me to her breezy, inattentive approach to operating a vehicle. My sister was brilliant, but living her entire life in Manhattan without access to a car did not a skilled driver make. "Fine," she sighed. "But you're taking Dad's car. I'm not riding around in that death trap."

"It's not a death trap," I snapped. "Subarus are some of the safest cars on the market. Haven't you seen the commercials? Plus I'm not strapping a tree to the roof of Dad's Benz. He'll kill both of us."

"Fair point. But we're listening to Christmas music, then."

As I navigated the winding, slick roads, Elena flipped from station to station, finally settling on one promising a solid hour of commercial-free holiday favorites. Great.

"The pass better be open," I muttered, more to myself than to Elena, as we approached the road taking us from Jackson into Idaho. Occasionally the Teton Pass was closed down due to inclement weather. Although, maybe if it was closed, I could forget this whole Christmas tree mission and get back to my regularly scheduled fireplace brooding.

"It will be. There isn't that much snow."

The landscape outside was a blur of green and white. Heavy snowflakes drifted down from a mottled slate sky onto a dark mass of swaying pines. An occasional powerful gust of wind kicked up glimmering swirls of powder. I gripped the wheel harder as the car slid on a patch of ice. The defroster was no match for the frigid temperatures.

"Ooh, I love this song!" Elena turned the dial on my radio to blast "Do They Know It's Christmas?" by Band Aid.

I balked and tore my eyes away from the road to desperately change the station. "No way."

"Come on!" Elena whined, deftly flicking right back to the offending song. "This song is awesome. It kinda takes me back."

"Okay, for one, you were born way after this song came out. And it's offensive as hell. It presents this totally monolithic image of African nations and codes the entire continent as deficit and needy. It's such white savior bullshit."

I could feel Elena's incredulous stare. "*Dio mio,* Mikah. Not everything has to be so serious."

Gripping the wheel even tighter, I rolled my eyes. "No, but it's worth unpacking—"

"Unpacking? It's a Christmas song, bro. You really find a way to overthink everything, don't you? Please don't analyze the music to death."

"Some of us *like* analyzing. I mean, it used to be my job and all," I teased. Elena tended to get irritated with my endless desire to nitpick and evaluate. She simply charged through life, absorbing what she wanted and eschewing the things she found unnecessary. I envied her.

We drove for a few more miles in silence. Well, not in silence. I had to endure the rest of the offensive holiday atrocity in addition to "Feliz Navidad," that weird, kind-of-metal version of "Carol of the Bells," and a truly awful rendition of "Santa Baby." Finally, though, my sister piped up to instruct me to turn off onto a dirt road marked with a small wooden sign welcoming us to Haskell Farms. I groaned.

When I eased the car to a halt in the gravel driveway, the place was deserted. Nothing but blowing snow, a drafty barn made of graying wood, and the icy wind cutting through my jacket as we stepped out of the car. It was eerily silent, and I almost missed the aggressive cheer of the Christmas music. Almost. All I wanted was to go home, curl up with a book, and forget everything. Although, I realized with a jolt, I had no idea where home was. Not my apartment back in Cambridge. I'd broken the lease at the beginning of November before selling off most of my belongings and hauling the rest to my dad's place. Home wasn't my mother's sprawling penthouse in SoHo, where my childhood bedroom had been transformed into a well-appointed office. And certainly not Josh's cramped, messy studio in San Francisco, where I'd never quite felt at ease.

"Um, are they even open?" I asked, not bothering to mask my irritation.

"That's what I'm looking at," Elena mumbled, eyes locked on her phone as she scrolled. "Google says they opened fifteen minutes ago. But the coverage out here sucks, so I can't get their actual website to load."

I was about to climb back into the driver's seat and steer us to any nursery or grocery store boasting even the sorriest of Christmas trees, when I was unceremoniously knocked to the ground. Frigid water and mud immediately soaked every inch of my clothing. I struggled to make sense of why the hell I was sprawled on the gravel. A large, wet tongue dragged over my face. Unaware I'd clamped my eyes shut, I cracked them open to find an enormous dog standing over my body, snuffling into my neck and pawing at my chest. It was so cute—with dopey eyes and silky brown, black, and white fur—I couldn't even be angry that I'd been slammed onto the cold, slushy driveway. My fingers tangled into the dog's coat, and a startled laugh erupted from my throat.

"Moose!" A low male voice sounded from a distance, and I tried to crane my neck to place the speaker. Not wanting to look like a total moron in front of some Idaho farmer dying to label me as a stuck-up city boy, I attempted to catch my breath. The dog had totally knocked the wind out of me. Elena was laughing in a wholly unhelpful way.

"Sorry." A big hand, rough and dotted with silver-white scars, enveloped mine and hauled me to my feet. I turned, brushing at my soaked clothes and struggling to shrug off my humiliation. But when I lifted my gaze from the ground to the man in front of me, I froze. He was exactly the kind of guy I would silently lust over but would never work up the courage to talk to. He had windswept dark blond hair, surprisingly warm blue eyes, and an almost unfairly perfect square, stubbled jaw. And he was huge, a towering wall of bulk clad in a brown Carhartt jacket and faded jeans. But, somehow, he wasn't intimidating. The man seemed to radiate a kind of earthy calm, like the molecules around him vibrated at a lower frequency. I could feel my mouth going a little slack as his eyes flicked from me to the dog, and a tiny smirk twitched his full lips. Before I could continue gawking at him, though, Elena stepped forward, extending her hand and beaming.

"Hi! We saw a flyer saying you sell Christmas trees?" Her voice had shifted from its usual slightly pestering tone to something softer. Was she flirting? I wanted to tell her to back off.

The man nodded at my sister. "Yes, ma'am. We have twenty-five acres of forest." He jabbed his thumb in the direction of an expanse of snow-dusted evergreens. "Any tree tagged with a white blaze is yours to cut down. It's seventy dollars."

"Perfect. And you can help us get it strapped to the car?"

For some reason I wanted to protest, to prove to this broad-shouldered hulk of a stranger that I could take care of it, despite the fact that I was easily a half foot shorter than him and at least fifty pounds lighter. When I chanced a look at him again, his eyes were on me, scanning over my wreck of an outfit. I was shivering hard and tried to relax my muscles and unclench my jaw.

"You want some dry clothes?" he asked, shoving his big hands into the pockets of his coat. "Sorry Moose knocked you over like that. He's not usually so wild with strangers." The dog wagged his tail like he knew he was the topic of conversation.

"Nah," I said breezily. "I'm good."

Elena scoffed, and I shot her what I really hoped was a withering look.

"My place is right over there. I can get you guys some hot chocolate, and you can warm up. It's no problem."

"Hot chocolate sounds fantastic," Elena agreed before I could even open my mouth to speak.

We followed the man for about five minutes, crunching over frozen grass. The farm was sprawling, with two barns, a modest ranch-style house, a greenhouse, and snow-cloaked fields that seemed to be largely plowed under for the winter. As we walked, Elena fired off a series of weirdly astute questions about organic farming, and the man answered her with earnest enthusiasm. I felt immediately like a sullen third wheel, hating myself for being jealous of Elena's ability to bond easily with new people. Then a small log cabin came into view, and my attitude shifted. The house looked like something on one of those Christmas popcorn tins. Smoke billowed from a stone chimney toward the winter-white sky. The railings of the wide porch were trimmed with juniper and pine sprigs. Icicles glittered along the eaves, and heavy drifts of snow coated the roof.

"Come on in," the man said, tugging open the substantial wooden door. I stumbled as I yanked off my boots, and the man's large hand gripped my shoulder, holding me steady. Heat coursed through my veins that had nothing to do with the blazing woodstove in the corner. My head spun as I glanced around the cabin. Hopefully I didn't have a concussion from my skull slamming into the driveway. But I figured the dizziness was just because the place was so damn perfect. If the outside of the cabin was dark and rustic, the inside was dreamy and light. Everything was whitewashed and clean, but still somehow cozy. The furniture was mismatched but well maintained. Inviting. The plaid sofa looked like the ideal place to nap or tuck my feet under me as I disappeared into a favorite novel. The rough-hewn walls were largely devoted to wide windows framing views of the snow-dusted forest and fields beyond. The scent of fresh-cut wood and coffee mingled with the snap of cold air from outside.

"Wow, this place is great." Elena followed the guy into the kitchen area as he set a gleaming kettle onto the stove's blue flame. He shrugged in response. I was still standing in the doorway, arms wrapped tight around myself. His clear, blue eyes kept flicking over me, and I started to worry I had mud all over my face or something.

"Do you have a bathroom?" I asked, immediately wanting to punch myself in the face. *Of course he has a bathroom.* The man's mouth twitched into a tiny smile again, and heat crept up my neck and into my cheeks.

"Yup. I'll grab you some dry clothes. Here—" I trailed behind him as he led me down a short hallway.

Darting into the bathroom and locking the door behind me, I didn't even allow myself to glance in the mirror as I scrubbed my face and hands with hot water from the tap. The bathroom was tiny but tidy—everything scoured clean and set in its place. A small, nosy part of me wanted to rummage through the unfairly gorgeous farmer's medicine cabinet and figure out something, anything, about him. Thankfully a soft knock startled me, saving me from myself. When I pulled the door open, the man pressed a bundle of neatly folded clothing into my hands. Our fingers brushed, driving a hot shock down my spine. Desire rushed through me, and I seemed to lose all ability to think rationally. I could feel myself blushing.

"Hot chocolate's ready whenever you are." He held eye contact for a tremulous moment, then looked down at the floor, smiling softly and rubbing the back of his neck.

Although he was being nothing but kind, a sharp, almost desperate longing twisted in my stomach. Homesickness for a place that didn't exist. I gave him a curt nod and hurried to strip out of my filthy clothes.

There was no way the flannel pants and long-sleeved T-shirt he'd given me would fit, but the fabric was soft and warm, as though he'd just pulled the clothes from the dryer. I cinched up the waistband of the pants and pushed up the shirtsleeves as best I could so I didn't look like a rag doll wandering back into the living room. A quick glance in the small mirror above the sink revealed that I did, unfortunately, look ridiculous in the baggy clothes.

Elena and the man were sitting on the couch, chatting amiably and sipping from steaming mugs as I shuffled down the hall. His voice was low and soft, a soothing rumble like thunder. I heard my name and something about me spending time out here after losing my job. *Wow, thanks for making me look good, El.* As I rounded the corner, my foot caught on the hem of the pants, and they slid down my hips. My cheeks burned. Fuck Christmas trees.

"HE was really cute, huh?" Elena raised her voice over a somewhat decent cello rendition of "Silent Night." Of course she would talk through the one Christmas song I could tolerate. And of course she would try to force me to discuss the nameless, probably straight, definitely gorgeous farmer.

"I guess." I fixed my attention on the road ahead, trying and failing to ignore the way my stomach flipped and my throat tightened at the mere mention of him. Desperately I tried to rationalize my overblown reaction as simple embarrassment at barely being able to stay upright in the guy's presence. But I knew what desire felt like: the buzzing heat, the intense curiosity, the inability to stop picturing his hand clasping mine as he pulled me off the snowy ground. I needed to clear my head, but it was hopeless. I was still wearing his clothes, enveloped in him. The clean smell of his fabric softener filled the small cabin of my car, mixing with the scent of pine from the holiday greenery Elena insisted we needed. The clothes, while way too big, were undeniably cozy. I couldn't remember the last time I'd worn anything so comfortable. Had I been alone and not navigating the twists of an impossibly icy road, I would have lifted the hem of the T-shirt to my nose, would have breathed him in.

My sister snorted and shook her head. "Come on, just because Josh turned out to be a cheating idiot asshole doesn't mean you can't admit some random, undeniably handsome dude is hot. Crushing on cute strangers is, like, my bread and butter."

Crush. I let the word swirl through my mind like the snowflakes spinning through the air outside. A crush was okay, right? A one-sided, short-lived crush. I could allow myself a little bit of harmless fun after the pathetic failure that had been my relationship with Josh. Of course, there was a chance I would actually have to talk to the hot farmer again tomorrow when I brought back his clothes. Then what? I imagined his big arms wrapping around me, the sound of that low voice in my ear. The feeble stream of tepid air blowing from the dashboard vent did little to heat up the car, but I was suddenly uncomfortably hot. Desperate for any distraction, I turned up the volume on the radio, the motion mindless and immediately regrettable.

"Hell. Yes." Elena turned the dial to blare Mariah Carey's "All I Want for Christmas Is You" loud enough that I was pretty sure the song echoed over the peaks of the Tetons and all the way back to the farm.

Damn if I didn't have to try really hard to hide my smile the whole way home.

Chapter Two

Matt

I TAPPED my foot along with the smooth notes of Elvis warbling "Blue Christmas." My hands were busy hanging my mismatched collection of ornaments on the small tree I'd cut down for myself, but my mind was firmly fixated on that mess of soft dark hair and those smoldering brown eyes framed by irresistibly long lashes. That wide, pretty mouth.... *No.*

Rolling my shoulders, I focused on the spruce boughs, making sure I put the heavier ornaments on the thicker branches. It seemed pointless to put up a tree since I was really the only person who would see it. But it felt wrong not to decorate for the holidays. Besides, before he left yesterday, Mikah had mumbled something about coming back to return my clothes, so maybe he would see the tree too. Maybe he'd even stick around to drink his cup of hot chocolate this time. He'd barely said two words as I helped him and his sister cut down a huge blue spruce and tether it to the roof of his beat-up car. He'd seemed standoffish, clearly irritated as he clomped after us through the forest, looking far too adorable in my oversized coat and clothes. His sister had chatted nonstop. I liked her. But not as much as I'd immediately liked him. I couldn't seem to forget the hitch of his breath or the way his ample lips had fallen open when our fingers brushed. And there was no way my mind was letting go of the image of that tight expanse of creamy skin when my flannel pants slipped down over the jutting bones of his hips.

Moose lay snuggled up on the couch, eyeing me with a *pull yourself together* expression. A rustle of footsteps sounded outside, and a small smile bloomed on my face. That was fast. It hadn't even been twenty-four hours since my dog unceremoniously hurtled Mikah into a puddle of muddy slush. But no knock came at the door. Instead it banged open, revealing not Mikah but John, my older brother, looking harried and talking a mile a minute.

"Dude, what the hell are you doing in here? It's nine. We have customers. Holiday rush, bro."

I glanced at the wall clock. *Damn it.* I'd been so busy mentally running my fingers over Mikah's soft mouth and wondering if that rumpled hair was as silky as it looked that I'd totally lost track of time. Typically winters were quiet at the farm. Other than going to an indoor farmer's market once a week to sell overwintered root vegetables and the small selection of greens and herbs we cultivated in the greenhouse, we spent most of the winter repairing equipment, taking care of overdue paperwork, and planning for the hectic seasons ahead. But things had gotten a whole lot busier since a bolt of inspiration struck my brother, and John had decided to start charging folks to cut down some of the evergreens in the forest for the holidays. It was a good idea, and yesterday's Black Friday tidal wave of cash had been nice, but I sort of missed the solitude of the wind whipping through the trees and the blank stretch of nothing but snow for miles.

"Sorry." I gave the tree a final once-over. It looked nice, encircled in white lights and dotted with colorful ornaments mostly made by John's eight-year-old daughter, Abby. I smiled before switching off the music and following my brother outside.

The air was frigid, the kind of biting cold that immediately pricked every inch of skin and tightened every cord of muscle. The whine of a chainsaw carried over the white spread of frozen fields.

"You okay, man?" John asked as we stomped over to the barn. A few cars sat along the driveway, but no battered navy Subaru was among them. No sign of Mikah.

I nodded vaguely. "Yup."

John didn't seem convinced. "You still bummed about that Nick dude?"

A low groan rumbled from my throat. John was so damn nosy about my love life. About a year earlier, I'd started chatting with a guy named Nick on a farming forum, and it turned out we were both gay. He was closeted and having a hard time with it, but incredibly sweet, and we'd hit it off almost immediately, emailing back and forth and texting. What started as idle small talk had quickly escalated to sexting, then video chats, then long phone calls that often ended with both of us falling asleep as we lamented the distance separating us. It had fizzled out after about ten months, though. Nick was undeniably gorgeous and so earnest, it had sometimes made my chest ache. But he was also undeniably out of reach, over two thousand miles away in Upstate New York. I still missed him sometimes, missed having someone to laugh with at the end of the day. I missed the undeniable pull to slot him into my life. And yeah, okay, I missed getting off, even if everything had been virtual.

"Nope." My gaze lifted to the wide expanse of clear blue sky. I loved days like this, the air bracing and crisp, the sharp peaks of the Tetons jutting toward feathery white clouds. Releasing a long breath, I let all the thoughts drain from my mind. My shoulders relaxed.

But John had other ideas and kept pressing. "Why don't you go out to Salt Lake City or something for New Year's? Hit up some of the bars. Or give that ski instructor a call. What was his name?"

"Nah," I said, still sticking with monosyllables. While I appreciated my brother's support, sometimes he was a little too enthusiastic. And invasive. And involved. Anytime he encountered a guy he even thought might be queer, John started mentally drafting the seating charts for our eventual wedding.

"My husband botherin' you, Matt?" Katie emerged from the barn, long black hair braided down her back. Abby followed close on her mother's heels, one of the red bows we used for the wreaths stuck to the middle of her forehead.

I shrugged while John scoffed. "I'm not bothering him." He jutted his chin indignantly. "He seems kinda down today, don't you think?"

Katie rolled her eyes at her husband. "Um, he seems fine. Why don't you worry about the folks who got their saw stuck in a tree trunk?" She shook her head at me in playful apology.

John bounded away, his broad back retreating toward the tree line. As irritating as my brother could be, I was undeniably grateful to have him. The two of us had relied on each other growing up: pushing each other to keep our grades from slipping, forging our parents' signatures on permission slips, making sure there was enough food in the fridge.

"Are you okay, though?" Katie asked, her narrow brown eyes locking intently on my face.

I chuckled. "You two are worse than a couple of brood hens. I'm fine. Holiday blues or whatever."

Katie patted my arm fondly. "You need to cool it with the Elvis in that cabin. Maybe try a little Mariah Carey for a change."

A laugh rumbled in my chest as I started wrapping twine around one of the freshly cut trees. Katie pointed me in the direction of the car I was supposed to tie it to, an immaculate black Range Rover, and informed me that the tree's new owners were now wandering around the farm, taking photos and spooking the horses.

Letting my mind drift again as I worked, I wondered whether Mikah had worn my clothes for long or if he'd shed them as soon as he got home, tossing everything in a heap on the floor. But an image of him stretching out in bed, my T-shirt rucking up over his flat stomach, had my mouth going dry. Thankfully the crunch of gravel under tires pulled me from my increasingly dirty thoughts. I grinned to myself when the navy Subaru Forester shuddered to a halt. Mikah was back. And he'd come by himself.

"Can you take care of that one?" Katie gave my arm a quick, hard squeeze. "Abby and I should go help out Mr. and Mrs. Los Angeles over there before they get themselves killed." She jabbed her thumb at the couple in question. They were now precariously balanced on top of the buck-rail fence surrounding the paddock and trying to take a selfie. I laughed again and nodded. But bright excitement fizzed in my stomach. I kept my gaze trained down on the Douglas fir and carefully unspooled the twine. Every footstep of Mikah's made my heart race a little more. When a pair of black boots kicked up the snow next to me, I glanced up, trying to keep my expression neutral.

"Hey." Mikah raked his fingers through his tousled curls. I cleared my throat to hide the fact that I wanted to groan as the scent of his hair drifted down to me: citrus and rich coffee and amber.

"Hey." I stood and wiped my hands on my jeans. Jesus, just looking at him had my skin burning and tingling with need. I could tell he was uncomfortable, though, shifting from foot to foot and shoving his hands deep into the pockets of his oversized green raincoat. Did the guy not own a single seasonally appropriate article of clothing? I wanted to pull him into my arms and hold him until he was warm. Instead, I focused my attention on the small canvas tote bag looped around his slender forearm.

He followed my gaze to the bag and seemed to spring back to life. "Oh, uh, right. Your clothes. Thanks again for loaning them to me. I washed everything." His jaw set tight as he stared out at the paddock.

I accepted the bag, wishing all the while he hadn't washed the clothes. The thought of his scent clinging to the shirt as I pulled it over my head did nothing to diminish my growing arousal. A tight thread of silence stretched out between us. I knew I had to say something or he would leave.

"You okay, then?" I asked. "Moose didn't hurt you?"

A small smile played over Mikah's gorgeous mouth. And now I couldn't seem to tear my eyes away from his lips. "I'm fine." He gave a small shrug. "Well, thanks again for all your help yesterday. And for the tree. My stepmom's thrilled with it."

"Yup. No problem." I desperately grasped at straws, trying to figure out some way to get him to stick around, even for a few minutes. "You never drank your hot chocolate yesterday. Want some now?"

That tiny smile again. Then an almost imperceptible nod. "Sure. If it's cool with your, um, wife." I followed his gaze to Katie, who now appeared to be conducting a full-on photo shoot for the couple by the paddock. Wife? I shook my head.

"Sister-in-law. But, yeah, it's fine. She and my brother can handle things for a few minutes. One sec, let me get this tied to those folks' car." I gestured down to the tree. As I hurried through the task, I let myself speculate wildly about Mikah. His sister had mentioned they grew up in New York City and that Mikah was taking some time to get himself together after losing a teaching job he'd loved. Idly, I wondered what grade he'd taught, which subject. I was lucky to have the farm, because I couldn't imagine having to scramble to make ends meet after losing out on work I cared about. Unfortunately she hadn't given me any hints about his sexuality or relationship status. And I definitely wasn't about to ask. But the hot spark that passed between us when we touched yesterday had me desperate to at least investigate.

"Okay." I tested the ropes on the car before nodding in the direction of my cabin.

We had just started walking across the field when a harsh voice cut across the driveway. "Excuse me. Sir? I'd like to pay for this now." Glancing back in the direction of the barn we'd turned into a makeshift holiday store, I had to suppress an audible groan. In the few minutes since Mikah had arrived, about six more cars had pulled up. A tall blonde woman clutched a bundle of juniper boughs in one hand and a fancy leather wallet in the other.

"Sorry, one second," I called back to her before turning to Mikah, hoping like hell he'd stick around. "My door's unlocked if you want to wait in my cabin. This'll only take a second."

"Um." He bit his lip nervously, and I tried yet again not to stare at his mouth. "I can help out if you want." His pretty brown eyes flicked to a large family arguing as they struggled to secure their tree to the roof of their minivan.

I grinned and clapped him on the shoulder, maybe a little too hard, because he swayed on his feet. I pulled away reluctantly. Even beneath that weird giant raincoat, I could feel the fine, delicate bones of his shoulder under my hand. "Yeah, thanks, man. Cash box is in the barn on the table in the corner. It's open... but I'll warn you, it's gonna be pretty disorganized. You can handle that until Katie comes back from the field. There should be a price list in there somewhere. Then hot chocolate. Okay?" If the guy had been a teacher, I was pretty sure he could manage John's haphazard collection of loose change and crumpled bills stuffed into the old steel box we brought to the markets.

"Wait—what? Alone? What if I, like, rob you?" As soon as the words left his mouth, Mikah blushed hotly, like he regretted voicing the thought.

"Was that your plan all along? To rob the family Christmas tree farm?" I was teasing, but Mikah shook his head hard.

"Shit. No. Sure, I can do that."

"Thanks. I trust you." And with *that* weird comment, I turned toward the blonde lady, who now looked like she might actually choke me if she had to wait another second, and told her to follow Mikah into the barn to pay.

After helping to strap trees to three different cars and earning twenty dollars in tips for my trouble, I found Mikah alone in the barn. He was examining the holiday greenery Katie had arranged in tin buckets tied to a twig trellis that she'd interwoven with white lights. I had no clue how she came up with all this: creative displays at the market, cute logos for the pickles and jams I made, and now the cutesy holiday stuff. I was thankful for her efforts, though, because three people yesterday had commented on how pretty the arrangement was and talked about posting pictures of it on Instagram. The display really did look nice, but it had nothing on the man standing next to it. When Mikah's eyes landed on me, he grinned, a smile so bright and warm, it transformed his entire face. He was beautiful, sure, but smiling so openly, he was too damn adorable. Quickly, though, he rearranged his features into a quizzical expression and held up a large bundle of mistletoe.

"What is this stuff? Like, five people bought it. It's expensive as hell." He spoke quickly, his head tipping to the side a little as he examined the delicate white berries and yellow-green leaves.

"Mistletoe," I said, working hard to keep my voice even. Had he really never seen it before? City folks were weird.

Mikah dropped the plant as if two of its tiny leaves had closed around his finger and bitten him. I didn't miss the small intake of breath or slight pink flush of his cheeks. The space between us suddenly felt like way too much and way too little at the same time. Never in my life had I experienced such an immediate, visceral attraction to someone. But it felt like more than a physical pull. It felt like connection. I wanted so much: wanted to pull him close, wanted to feel his soft curls as they slid between my fingers, wanted to trace the fine lines of his jaw. What I didn't want was to freak him out.

I cleared my throat. "Don't worry. Not gonna try to kiss you or anything." The words tumbled out of my mouth before I could stop them. Why did I keep saying such weird shit? Besides, kissing him had been on my mind pretty much nonstop since yesterday. I rubbed the back of my neck, which, despite the frigid wind whistling through the slats in the barn, burned almost painfully hot.

"Um." Mikah's eyes flashed wide and fixed hard on the cash box. "So, yeah. I don't think I fucked anything up. I remembered from yesterday that the trees are seventy, right? And I, uh, followed this very official document for everything else." He held up the pricing sheet, written out by Abby with glittery crayon on a piece of green construction paper. That adorable, sweet smile was back on Mikah's face.

A hard gust of wind slammed into the barn, and Mikah wrapped his arms around himself, grabbing his biceps tight. There was no way that damn jacket was protecting him from the cold on a day like this. His fingertips were white, and I realized with a sharp bolt of worry that he was shivering. My desire to stand around and flirt in the drafty barn evaporated. I needed to get him warmed up.

"Hot chocolate?" My voice sounded rough even to my own ears.

"Are you sure you have time? It seems like you guys are pretty busy today."

Aside from the distant groan of the saws and the ever-present murmur of the wind, it was quiet. I shrugged. "I have time." I would gladly give up the extra cash and face my brother's good-natured irritation if it meant spending even five extra minutes with Mikah.

After a moment he nodded, murmuring a muted "okay."

Mikah followed me at a distance. I glanced back at him, realizing there was a good chance I was making him uncomfortable. I knew my size and taciturn nature sometimes intimidated people. And the fact that I kept gawking at him probably didn't help. So I tried some small talk, slowing my steps so he could catch up. "Your sister told me you're from Manhattan?"

"Yeah." Mikah's voice was soft and his arm bumped mine as we walked side by side through the newly fallen snow. "We grew up there. But I moved to Boston for college and stayed. I guess I liked it better than New York. It's a little calmer. Especially Cambridge. Plus I got a job with Boston Public Schools right after finishing my master's. But then in August, I found out my position got cut. The district laid off, like, a hundred teachers. I was one of them." He pressed his lips firmly together and shook his head like he was scolding himself for saying too much. His eyes were wary when they flicked to mine.

Okay, so my attempts at light, pleasant conversation were a failure. "What did you teach?" I asked, pushing open my front door and shrugging out of my coat.

"Creative writing and journalism. And one section of AP Lit. But since I mostly taught electives...." He dragged his finger over his throat.

"Damn. That sucks, man."

Mikah shrugged. "Yeah."

He stared down at the floor, arms crossed over his narrow chest. I couldn't tell if he was dying to leave or if he just didn't mind the quiet. Or maybe he was worried I was about to murder him. In an attempt to ease the awkward silence that slammed down between us like a metal gate, I turned on some music, *Christmas with Elvis and The Royal Philharmonic Orchestra*. The noise seemed to calm Mikah, and he drifted over to the low bookcase crammed with all my dad's old CDs. It was mostly classic country: Patsy Cline, Hank Williams, Johnny Cash, George Jones. And of course Elvis. Every single album the King of Rock and Roll ever released. I set a pan on the stove and rummaged around in the cabinet for cocoa powder and marshmallows. No instant stuff today.

"You like Elvis, huh?" Mikah asked, a smile in his voice. I smiled too. People loved to tease me about my Elvis obsession. But Elvis was the sound of good days. When I came home from school and heard "Jailhouse Rock" or "Heartbreak Hotel" blasting from the boom box in the living room, I knew my dad would be bright eyed, grinning, excited to ask me about my day. Sometimes he would put Elvis on while we worked in the garage, tuning up the tractor or messing around with carpentry projects. The music made me happy.

"Yup," I said, eyes raking over Mikah. His lithe frame was clad entirely in black: black jeans, thin black sweater, even his socks were black. I tried not to let myself stare at the perfect lines of his body as he bent down to brush his fingertips over the spines of the large collection of gardening books crowding the bottom shelf. His fingers were long, slim, elegant. I wondered idly if he played the piano.

"Elvis was my first crush," I murmured. Mikah's fingers stilled on the books. He turned to me, eyes wide. I refocused on stirring up the hot chocolate.

When I asked Mikah if he wanted marshmallows, he just nodded, looking dazed. And when we sat down, he scooted to the opposite end of the couch. Something deflated in my chest, but I quickly tried to shake it off. More light conversation, then he'd leave. I'd go back to my quiet routine. Wake up, exercise, eat, work, sleep, repeat. It was fine that way.

"So has your dad lived in Jackson long?" I asked, trying to cut the sudden tension in the room with more small talk.

Mikah gripped his mug with both hands, curling in on himself. I wondered if yet again I'd managed to stumble into a conversational minefield. Maybe I needed to work on my social skills.

Mikah's throat clicked in an audible swallow. "A few years," he said, very intent on inspecting my Christmas tree.

Once again the conversation faltered. I'd never been good at talking. But I wanted to learn more about this beautiful, adorably anxious man. Besides, the way Mikah flushed at the suggestion of kissing, the recognition in his eyes when I mentioned my crush on Elvis, I was starting to guess he was also somewhere on the queer spectrum. Selfishly, I wanted to know for sure—I just plain wanted him. I also wanted him to be comfortable. Even if he might be into guys, that didn't mean he would necessarily be into me. All of my stupid inner turmoil bubbled up into my throat, and I groaned. Fuck. I didn't know how to do this.

Color rose to Mikah's cheeks, and he lifted his gaze to mine, glancing at me through inky lashes. He really was adorable. Hot tension arced between us, and my whole body clenched with need at the thought of his full lips against mine. Too bad I hadn't brought some of that damn mistletoe with me. Taking a slow, deep breath, I decided honesty would be the best course of action. "I want to kiss you." I looked right at him.

Mikah's breath caught. He took a large gulp of hot chocolate, wincing like he'd burned himself. A tiny bit of marshmallow stuck to his full lower lip. Lust sluiced through me when his tongue darted out to lick it away.

"That okay?" I asked. The words came out low and rough. I cleared my throat. Mikah nodded slowly. "C'mere." I patted the couch next to me. He slid over, clearly tentative, his eyes still locked with mine.

With equal trepidation I lifted my thumb to his mouth, brushing over it softly. His skin was warm and flower-petal soft. Then his tongue was on my finger, and electric pleasure thrummed over every inch of my skin. One touch and I was aching for him as his lips closed around the very tip of my thumb. His shoulders dropped, and he gasped, an audible release of the tension he'd been radiating since he got out of his car. Mikah smiled a small, almost victorious smile. Then he closed the rest of the distance between us, and his lips brushed the corner of my mouth, the contact still a little cautious.

"Please," I breathed against his lips, my mouth so dry I could barely grind the word out.

I was frozen on the spot, desire rooting me to the couch. All I could do was stare at him, a little surprised but a lot turned-on as he climbed onto my lap, straddling me. He kissed me again, this time hot and hungry. No one had ever kissed me like this, so open and needy and... present. Now, Mikah was holding nothing back. His lips were plush and smooth against mine, and as his tongue slipped into my mouth, my whole body flushed with delicious pleasure. My brain finally caught up and my hands flew to his slim hips, locking him against me as he pressed openmouthed kisses all over my jaw, my ear, my throat, then back to my lips. The intensity of his need was unmistakable in every tiny sigh and soft gasp.

"Oh God, sorry. Shit. I, uh, kind of lost control there for a second." Mikah released a shaky laugh and nuzzled his face into the curve of my neck. The intimacy of the gesture only ratcheted up my desire further, lodging dry heat in my throat and pulling a rough growl from my chest. I was dizzy with my need to touch him, to tangle my fingers into his hair, to rub my palms over his skin, to kiss every inch of him.

His lips curved up in a smile against my throat. "So," he whispered, and his breath was a feather dragging against my skin. "I don't actually know your name."

As gently as possible, I clutched his narrow shoulders and pushed him back so I could look in his eyes. They were hooded, long lashes fluttering and pupils blown out. "Matt," I said softly.

"Mikah," he returned, pointing to his chest, although I already knew. He leaned forward to skim his lips over mine. Finally I gave in to my desire to fist my hand into his messy dark curls. His hair was even softer than I'd imagined, and I gripped it hard, crushing our mouths together. The kiss deepened, both of us pressing on each other like we couldn't possibly get close enough. Mikah rolled his hips, rutting his hardness against me, and I trailed my hands down his back to hold him tight against my body.

"Whoa!" Our heads both snapped up at the gust of cold air and booming sound of John's voice that accompanied it. I slammed my head back against the couch and groaned as Mikah clambered off of me. "Sorry! Didn't mean to interrupt. I thought you were alone, dude." My stupid brother's dumb voice was heavy with mirth.

Mikah had actually thrown a pillow over his crotch like we were in high school. I couldn't help but grin. Giving his knee a quick, gentle squeeze, I made the appropriate introductions. Well, as appropriate as possible given the uncomfortable circumstances. "John, this is Mikah. Mikah, this idiot is my brother, John."

"Pleased to meet you." John inclined his head, doing his dumb charming cowboy routine. Mikah nodded but mostly looked like he wanted to die on the spot.

"Did you need something?" I asked through gritted teeth.

"Well, it's getting kinda busy out there. Could use your help." John looked suddenly sheepish. "But, um, I'll give y'all a minute." He yanked the door shut, and through the large front window I watched him dart back to the barn with an irritating spring in his step.

"Shit." Mikah huffed, wheeling on me. "I'm so sorry. Did he know?"

I nodded and traced my fingers over the fine line of his jaw, then over his lips again. They were damp and swollen. "Yeah. He knows I'm gay. He's probably in seventh heaven right now. Always trying to matchmake."

Mikah snorted; then we both dissolved into laughter. It felt good. I couldn't remember the last time I'd felt so at ease with someone who wasn't John or Katie.

"Sorry, though. I totally interrupted your day. And, honestly, I'd better head home. My older brother gets in tonight, and everyone's freaking out trying to get stuff ready. Luca's totally my dad's favorite kid." His wry expression seemed a little forced.

"Don't apologize. I'll take an interruption like this any damn time." I chucked him under the chin, and he rolled his eyes. Being with Mikah felt surprisingly natural, easy like slipping into a favorite wash-worn T-shirt. "Can I get your number maybe?" I asked, desperately hoping he'd say yes.

"Fuck yeah." Mikah beamed and wrenched his phone from his back pocket. I gave him my number, and he texted me so I had his, the distant buzz sounding in the pocket of my coat. "Do you want to hang out tomorrow, like maybe get a drink or something?" His nervousness was back, like maybe he was worried I would say no.

I knew that tomorrow the farm would likely be slammed with people hurrying to get trees and greenery, now that the holiday season had officially begun. I also could not have cared less about ditching all of my work duties to spend every possible minute with Mikah. "Yeah." I brushed his hair back from his face because I couldn't seem to stop touching him. "Do you like hiking?"

He made a seesaw motion with his hand, and I remembered that the guy didn't seem to own any functional winter clothing. "I'll try it," he hedged, looking incredulous.

"Okay." I heaved myself off the couch before tugging Mikah to his feet. I wanted to wrap my arms around him and never let him go. Instead I hurried to the entryway and handed him his impractical jacket. "Meet me at three at the Cache Creek Trailhead. And try to dress warm."

Chapter Three

Mikah

TINY bubbles fizzed around the translucent strips of orange zest. Catching my lower lip between my teeth, I scooped the pieces of candied citrus peel out of the simple syrup, then carefully arranged them on a sheet of waxed paper. Nonna had always insisted that good, homemade candied orange was the key to excellent panettone. This would be the first year she wasn't around to make the Christmas bread, since she had, unfortunately, decided to stay in Palermo to spend the holidays with my zia Paola and cousins. But even if Nonna wasn't going to be here, I wanted everything to be perfect. On a marble slab next to the sink, Elena rhythmically kneaded the egg-yellow dough, filling the kitchen with a buttery, yeasty aroma.

Our older brother, Luca, wandered in from the living room, dark hair perfectly slicked back, tapping away on his phone. "Any coffee left?" he asked, not looking up.

"No, Mikah drank the last of it." Elena threw me under the bus.

Now I'd have to struggle all over again with our dad's space-age espresso machine. I longed for the easy familiarity of my moka pot back home, the comforting sound of the coffee percolating on the stove. Then I remembered, yet again, that this faux-rustic mansion was my home for the time being. Not too bad, all things considered. But I still hated my dad's fancy coffee maker.

Popping one of the slightly cooled pieces of orange peel into my mouth snapped my mind right back to where I didn't want it to go. To the day before. To the way Matt's body had reacted to me licking the marshmallow off my lips. The sweetness lingering on his tongue. The way his strong hands had gripped my waist and tangled into my hair. The way he'd smelled like fabric softener and pine. The surprising trust he showed for me to help him out with his business even though he hardly knew me.

I splashed a little cold water from the sink on my face and patted my heated skin with a clean dishtowel. The last thing I needed was to get hard while hanging out in the kitchen with my siblings. Scratch that. The actual last thing I needed was to be thinking of Matt at all.

Last night had been restless: punching my pillow, rustling around in bed, thinking of what I might say and what he might say when we saw each other next. I was almost sick with wanting. Finally, failing to pause the looping reel of our kiss in my mind, I'd decided that I was going to cancel our date. If I was already obsessing over Matt to this degree after spending all of a collective hour in his presence, there was no way I could handle seeing him again. Having just emerged from the fog of heartbreak, I was terrified of intimacy, and I was fine with that fact, thank you very much.

As if Elena could read my mind, she glanced up from her steady kneading and pinned me with a long look. "What happened with the Christmas tree dude yesterday? You were gone for a while." Her perfect eyebrows arched toward her hairline.

Luca looked up from his phone. "Christmas tree dude? You already seeing someone, Mikah? Because you shouldn't rush into anything…." His broad shoulders tensed under his blazer. I had never seen my brother dress casually. Or act remotely calm. He'd always been overprotective and intense.

"Stai zitta," I hissed, shushing Elena and ignoring Luca altogether.

But my brother, undeterred, set his phone down and started efficiently preparing himself an espresso. He spoke with his back to me. "Dad says you've been sullen since you got here. And I don't blame you. The way Josh handled the breakup was bullshit. All I'm saying is you should take some time. You're only twenty-four. Relax. Go skiing. Get to know yourself again. You don't need to be jumping into a new relationship just a few months after you got dumped."

My stomach dropped at the mention of Josh's name. Dumped didn't even begin to describe what he'd done. But what word did one use to describe an abrupt radio silence after three years of dating, one of them a desperate attempt to make things work long-distance, followed by a curt letter detailing his engagement to someone else? I guess dumped would have to work.

"Luca, drop it." Elena's voice was gentle. But then she turned to me. "That guy was gorgeous. And he couldn't keep his eyes off you. Please, please tell me he, like, bent you over a hay bale and had his way with you."

My cheeks burned. "Jesus, El. You're disgusting." Actually, though, that sounded really hot. Or it would have if it weren't my damn sister saying it.

"Oh my God. Something did happen!" Elena clapped her hands together. "*Dimmi!*"

I threw my head back with an exasperated sigh. "We kissed, you weirdo. Whatever. It wasn't a big deal." Lie. I couldn't stop thinking about the perfect way our mouths had fit together.

Luca took a break from stirring sugar into his coffee to drag a hand over his trim beard. He and our father sported identical facial hair. And now he was also wearing the exact same all-knowing, patronizing expression our dad favored. Great. "Mikah," he began, and I half expected him to call me *caro* the way our mom did, "are you sure this is a good idea? You know you don't exactly have the best track record."

God, my family was never going to let me live down my romantic failures. I'd been a shy kid. So when I finally came out in high school and started dating Steven, everyone had been thrilled. He took me to concerts. We went to parties together and hung out with his friends in artfully shabby apartments in the Village. My family's joy had evaporated, however, when Steven came over for dinner, and they discovered he was a senior at NYU. I was seventeen and hadn't even seen anything wrong with the whole arrangement. I'd felt lucky he was interested in me. Between that debacle and the recent collapse of my relationship with Josh, I didn't really blame Luca for being concerned. Well, logically I didn't blame him. I was concerned enough for the both of us, though. I'd recently learned that opening up to someone was basically a recipe for disaster. Clenching my fists, I stared anywhere but my brother's face.

"You don't have to worry, because I'm not going to see him again." The embarrassment surging through me only made my voice sound brittle. I was already tired of talking about this. All I wanted to do was finish making the panettone and switch off my overheated brain, maybe lose myself in a book or go for a long run on the treadmill in the basement. Anything to get Matt out of my head.

"No?" Elena rested her hand on mine.

"No," I insisted. "I want to, but I'm not going to." That made perfect sense, right?

Now Luca had the dignity to look abashed. "Well, if you like him…."

"I do." *I can't fucking stop thinking about him.* Keeping the second admission to myself, I turned back to the recipe card printed with Nonna's spidery script, hoping neither of my siblings could see how hard I was blushing. My grandmother's handwriting brought a wave of cool comfort, reminding me of letters filled with gentle, encouraging words and practical advice. "But there's no point. If I see him again, I'll just like him more. Then it'll hurt worse when I go back to New York in January. Or when he decides he's not into me after all. So, yeah. No point. Not going hiking with him." I said this more to convince myself than my siblings.

Luca's face was a mask of exasperation, but Elena looked sympathetic and a little amused. "Yeah, okay, Mikah. That makes sense. You might like him, so you should avoid him. Super-reasonable." She laughed.

"It is!" I insisted. "I don't even live here. The whole thing would be a waste of time." My conviction was starting to fail, however.

"In what world is a sexy holiday fling a waste of time? I'm not saying you have to fall in love or something, but it wouldn't kill you to have a little fun. I would be all over that if the dude looked at me the way he was checking you out. And I don't even like guys that much." Elena's voice lilted. She bit the inside of her cheek. "So, hiking? That sounds, um, wholesome."

"Ugh. I know. I don't even have a warm enough coat."

Luca's irritation seemed to multiply. "Jesus, Mikah." Now he really sounded like our dad. "You lived in Boston. How do you not own a warm coat? It's not like you can't afford one."

Not wanting to admit I'd lost my heaviest coat, in addition to my dignity, at a bar after getting blackout drunk the night I received Josh's stupid breakup letter, I shrugged.

"Borrow my Canada Goose coat. And go on the damn date," Luca insisted. Then he picked up his phone and stalked out of the kitchen to make a call.

FOR the second time in as many days, I would be hanging out with Matt while looking like an extra in *Oliver Twist*. Like Matt, Luca towered over me and was significantly bulkier than I was. My brother tended to obsess over his body a little bit, spending tons of time at an expensive gym, working out with his personal trainer. So, naturally, his coat looked ridiculous on me.

"Don't say a word," I growled at Matt as I trudged through knee-deep snow to where he leaned against the sign marking the trailhead. His eyes were locked on me, steady and warm, making my heart falter in my chest and blood rush to my cheeks. And he looked unfairly gorgeous with his close-cropped blond hair, perfect scruff, and brown work coat, like he'd sprung to life from the pages of some kind of rugged outdoor outfitters catalogue. Next to him, Moose snorted and pawed at the snow. I was thankful the dog didn't go for an encore performance of his tackling routine. Instead he gave a happy bark and wagged his fluffy tail.

"I brought an extra coat for you." Matt patted the hiking pack on his back. "But it looks like you found something warm enough. Kinda big, though." The damn smirk reappeared on his lips. I wanted to kiss it away.

"It's my brother's coat. He's a sasquatch like you, so...."

Matt chuckled, and we started along the trail. Thankfully the snow was tamped down with footprints, and the path was well maintained. "How many siblings do you have?" he asked after a moment of walking in pleasant silence. I got the impression that he, like me, wasn't big on idle chatting.

"Only two. Elena and Luca, my older brother. He's an attorney. A senior partner at the LA office of my dad's firm. He can be... a lot, but he's a good guy."

"I liked your sister. She said she's an engineer?" Matt's strides were so long, I had to hurry to match his pace. So naturally I slipped on a snow-covered root and bumped into him. I was making a great impression so far. Matt chuckled and ghosted his fingers over my cheek before continuing down the trail more slowly.

"Uh-huh. She studied civil engineering at the Cooper Union. She's wicked talented too. Super into sustainable design and always going on and on about infrastructure and stuff. Right after graduating she got hired at some eco-friendly start-up… to be honest I'm not really sure what she does. The hours are insane, but she works from home most of the time. I'm proud of her, though."

"That's so cool." Matt seemed to perk up. "Must have been nice for her to be able to stay close to home and work with such interesting faculty."

I was startled he'd even heard of Elena's school. Then I felt like a pretentious jerk for being surprised. Just because Matt was a farmer from Idaho didn't mean he was unaware of institutions of higher education. But the Cooper Union was fairly small and kind of niche.

"Yeah," I said slowly, trying to figure out a tactful way of asking why the hell he seemed to know so much about the school. But he supplied the answer before I could even ask the question.

"I wanted to be a mechanical engineer when I was in high school. It was a total pipe dream obviously, but I thought about applying there because of the scholarship program and stuff." He seemed a little embarrassed, as if he were admitting a dark secret rather than an adolescent career goal.

"That's awesome. What did you end up studying?" Immediately I loathed myself for asking the question. I sounded like a snob, subtly digging to find out where he went to school so I could slot him into a bullshit status hierarchy. Matt and I were walking side by side now, so in an attempt to distract him, I grabbed his hand and ran my fingers over his rough knuckles. His hand was warm and heavy in mine.

"Nothing. Didn't go to college. Kept on working the farm." Coming to a sudden halt, he threaded our fingers together and then hauled me up against him, holding me in his big arms. Without thinking, I nuzzled into his chest. We had stopped in a small clearing, and the wind whistled through the trees. I let my eyes drift shut as I breathed in the woodsmoke smell of Matt's coat.

"Beautiful here, huh?" The words rumbled through his body.

My eyes snapped open. I'd been so hung up on Matt, I'd failed to take in our surroundings. But the forest was, indeed, beautiful. A vast unencumbered view stretched below us: snow-tipped pines, rolling foothills, and swirling clouds promising snow. The cold quieted everything; even the gusts of wind and the occasional tap of a woodpecker searching the bark of a nearby tree seemed muted. If I could, I decided I would stay here forever: secure in Matt's embrace, breathing him in, with nothing to disturb me but the occasional distant crack of a stick or the icy prickle of a snowflake working its way down the collar of my coat. I barely knew this man, but I already felt so safe in his arms. Comfortable. Like I could say anything and he would just reply with a soft smirk and a fast kiss.

"It really is. Do you come hiking here a lot?" I was literally making the weakest small talk known to man.

"Yup."

"I don't exactly do a lot of outdoorsy stuff." I was babbling. My voice had gone all weird and shaky because Matt's fingers were brushing my skin, pushing my hair back from my face. I felt like an exposed live wire, sparking each time he touched me. "Like, some of my friends in grad school were big into camping and stuff, going up to Vermont or New Hampshire on the weekends, but it wasn't my thing. I'll bet you were a Boy Scout or something, though."

A tiny wrinkle appeared between Matt's brows, and his lips pressed into a firm line. Then as quickly as the concerned expression appeared on his face, it lifted, like one of the clouds passing over the mountain peaks surrounding us. "Nah. Mostly did stuff around the farm. John and I went camping sometimes, though. Hiked a lot. Went fishing."

Moose raced ahead of us as we started back along the trail, Matt's hand still engulfing mine. He was so much taller than me, I had to imagine it was almost awkward for him to walk this way, but if it bothered him, he kept it to himself. Besides, I liked being close to him. Probably too much.

"So what kind of kid were you?" I asked, still apparently hell-bent on making dull small talk. I never did this. Throughout college and grad school I'd been nothing but irreverent in response to the boilerplate getting-to-know-you questions: where did you grow up, what do you do for fun, if you could have dinner with one person living or dead who would it be? But with Matt I wanted to know every single detail of his past and present. I actually wanted to know what his favorite book was. How he took his coffee. Did sleep find him easily, or did he toss and turn like I did.

"Normal, I guess. Super into vo-tech. Kept to myself." Matt shrugged his big shoulders, then glanced down at me, his lips quirking up. "I bet you were all goth, right? Real into poetry and music and stuff."

A laugh erupted from me. I hadn't even been original enough to dress goth in high school. My school had required us to wear uniforms, tidy red-trimmed navy blazers and starched white shirts. Unlike other kids who pushed the limits of the dress code, I went along with it, not caring enough to make waves. My weekend clothes had been designer samples my mom handpicked for me: cashmere sweaters, tailored jeans, artfully distressed T-shirts that cost far more than any swath of cotton ever should. I just put on the stuff I liked and left the rest in the fancy shopping bags in my closet for her to take back to the office.

"No, I was kinda weird. Quiet, gay as hell, worried all the time, obsessed with doing well in school. I didn't have a ton of friends to be honest. I was big into reading, though. English was always my best subject. I was even the editor of my school's literary magazine. Very cool stuff." I glanced up at Matt, at his solid frame and long limbs. "To be honest I'm kinda surprised to hear you weren't some star athlete. Like a linebacker or... okay, I don't know anything about sports."

Matt had gone tense again, and I was starting to get that maybe he didn't particularly like talking about his childhood. "I did play football. Stopped my junior year, though."

We'd turned off the main trail and were now descending a narrower path through dense forest. Moose bounded forward, the sound of his paws crushing over frozen snow a steady rhythm. Matt hadn't once stopped to look at the trail maps, and I realized I'd been following him blindly. He seemed so sure of where we were going, I didn't even think to question it. But the sky was already darkening a bit, and my skin prickled with a tiny flash of worry.

"Is it getting dark already?" My voice totally betrayed my anxiety.

Matt glanced up at the sky, now a deeper gray as the snow had started to fall in earnest. "Yup. Sun sets before five this time of year. But we'll be back to the trailhead soon. This path loops us back around to where we started."

I followed him and Moose through the silent woods, calm firmly back in place since Matt did actually seem to know the trails. I couldn't keep my eyes off him, and when he looked down and saw me staring, he just grinned. He seemed so solid and comfortable in his own skin, moving through the snow like he never second-guessed a single step.

Moose bounded alongside us, occasionally darting into the underbrush to sniff or dig, but otherwise sticking close. Every ten minutes or so, Matt would stop and kick at the snow with the tip of his boot. I had no earthly idea what he was doing. Marking the trail? Checking for tracks? But when he came to a dead halt and crouched down to brush powdery snow away from a clump of loose rocks, I finally had to ask what he was up to. In response he lifted a snow-damp brown and ochre rock, smooth and striated with blueish gray.

"Sandstone." Matt held the rock up, seeming to address it directly. "My niece, Abby, has a huge rock collection. Right now she's on a sandstone kick. This one's pretty nice, huh?" He slipped the rock into his coat pocket, patting it once as if ensuring it was tucked away safely. Something about the gesture was so tender and sweet. It was like Matt had been designed specifically to appeal to every one of my innermost desires. Big and burly? Check. Ruggedly handsome? Check. Surprisingly thoughtful and adorable? Double fucking check.

I was usually terrible at initiating physical affection, vacillating between bumbling conversation and getting tangled up in my own thoughts, but the desire to be close to Matt overwhelmed my usual self-consciousness. I leaned into his broad frame, pressing myself up and pulling him down to claim his mouth with mine. Matt's lips fell open with a soft moan, the kind of satisfied sound I imagined he might make upon biting into a perfectly ripe piece of fruit. My pulse raced, and I tugged him closer, slipping my tongue against his. I was surprised by my own desperation for contact, his skin, his mouth, his hands. Matt gripped my shoulders, firm and strong. My pulse quickened. But instead of hauling me against him, he gently pried me away. I whimpered, still thrumming with need.

"I like you." He grinned, and his voice warmed me straight through, like sinking into a hot bath.

All my words left me, and I stared at the path while my heart soared up to fly among the swirling snowflakes.

"You want to maybe get some dinner? No worries if you can't. I know you might have plans with your family. But it's getting pretty cold, and I'm starving. We're only about a ten-minute walk from where we parked. If you want, you can follow me into town. This place, Café Ines, is really good, and it's dog friendly." He scratched the top of Moose's head, not meeting my eye. It was probably the most Matt had spoken since we met.

"Yes," I said quickly. Now that I'd forced myself to go on this date, I was dreading us parting. Dreading the moment that Matt, like Josh, might decide I wasn't worth it. I didn't know if I could handle more heartbreak, more unanswered texts, more letting myself be vulnerable, only to feel like a complete fool. Already I knew I liked Matt too much. One more afternoon with him, and I'd let my fantasies shift from making out to waking up together.

My face burned despite the cold wind. I shivered at the thought of spending the night with Matt, laying my head on that broad chest, his heartbeat lulling me to sleep, soothing and steady like a metronome.

Chapter Four

Matt

"WHAT can I get you boys?" The waitress glanced between me and Mikah, eyebrows arching toward her blonde hairline.

Mikah's cheeks, already pink from the cold wind, flushed red. "Uh, sorry. I'll need a second." He scanned the menu while I placed my order for a Teton Amber Ale and fried chicken. Seeming distracted from the moment he followed Moose and me into the warm, softly lit restaurant, Mikah hadn't even looked at the menu. Since we sat down, he'd alternated between taking giant gulps of water, shredding his napkin, and glancing down at Moose where he lay under the table. I couldn't tell if the guy was nervous or just really wasn't into the date anymore. Maybe he'd been hoping for a fast hookup instead of dinner?

"And for you?"

"I'll do the gnocchi and the IPA, please." Mikah gave the waitress a polite smile and handed over his menu.

Her pen paused on her notepad, and her heavily lined eyes swept over Mikah's thin frame, clad in a slightly ratty gray sweater. "Can I get a real quick look at your ID?" She looked half-apologetic, half-suspicious as Mikah fumbled for his wallet and handed her a Massachusetts driver's license.

The moment she walked away, I couldn't resist the urge to tease Mikah. "You still get carded, huh? Hey, enjoy it while you can. I never get asked."

Mikah shook his head and sifted his fingers through his hair, pushing the tousled curls back from his face. With some effort I focused on our conversation instead of my very sudden, very strong desire to touch him. "Ugh. It happens all the fucking time. There's no way I look under twenty-one either." When I only shrugged in response, Mikah narrowed his eyes at me. "Wait, how old are you, anyway, Mr. I Never Get Carded?"

I barked out a laugh. "Twenty-nine. But even when I used to try and underage drink, I usually got away with it. Guess I always looked old or somethin'."

"Ooh, underage drinking, huh? You were definitely edgier than me. The only time I ever drank underage was when my mom bought some super-rare wine she wanted us to try for 'educational purposes.'" He made air quotes around the words. "That and a few times with my weirdo boyfriend."

I knew if I looked at Mikah, my feelings would be too plain on my face, so I fixed my attention on our surroundings. I definitely didn't want him to see how stupidly, irrationally possessive I got at the mention of this boyfriend. I wanted to rub Mikah's hunched shoulders and smooth the little wrinkle of concern between his eyebrows. Instead, I let my gaze travel from the twinkling white string lights stretched above the small bar to the sprigs of holly tucked among the bottles of wine and come to rest on the tiny fake Christmas tree shoved into a corner. It never failed to amuse me how quickly the town of Jackson transformed itself into a winter wonderland in the days after Thanksgiving. Christmas lights twined around the elk antler arches in the town square. Cheerfully decorated Christmas trees in the lobby in every hotel. Twangy versions of holiday music spilling out from every tourist store…. But who was this boyfriend, anyway? Okay, clearly trying to distract myself didn't work.

"Weirdo boyfriend?" My voice sounded gruffer than I wanted it to.

Mikah's full lips twisted to the side. "It's a dumb story, honestly." He paused, and I nodded, encouraging him to continue. "My senior year of high school, I auditioned for this spot at a conservatory. For piano. I used to be totally obsessed, but I wasn't quite good enough. I didn't get in. Anyway, at the audition I met this guy. I knew he was older. But I guess I thought he was at least around my age. He was actually there as an assistant or something. He asked me out for coffee, and we started dating. My first real boyfriend. Turned out he was studying music at NYU. Kind of a creep. Anyway, my family won't let me live it down. My brother especially. It was seven goddamn years ago, but he still acts like I'm a total moron when it comes to relationships. When I got dumped a few months ago, they all acted like I was going to fall apart. I mean, yeah, it sucked to find out in a fucking letter that my boyfriend had fallen in love with someone else. But really, I'm fine. Plus, it's kind of nice to have some time to figure out what I want to do next without having to take someone else into consideration, you know?" Mikah shook his head, looking suddenly sheepish. "And, talking about my relationship baggage is *so* not pleasant date conversation. Sorry. I guess I kind of suck at this." He looked down at where Moose snoozed under the table for a long moment. "Also, your dog is being so good. Did you train him yourself or is he, like, naturally calm?"

Trying to hide the warring anger on Mikah's behalf and amusement at his attempt to change the topic, I covered his hand with mine on the table. His skin was cold, and the tips of his fingers were white. I didn't know what to say, so I just shook my head. I was damn rusty at this whole dating thing. Well, okay, not so much rusty as totally inexperienced. My heart hammered in my chest as I realized that this was my first actual date with a man. Quick and dirty hookups with tourists and closeted ranchers didn't leave a lot of space for sharing a meal or conversation.

I glanced at Mikah, his eyes fixed on our joined hands. He was beautiful. But the beauty wasn't only in his lush mouth, straight eyebrows, and long delicate nose. It was more than the spill of long inky lashes over alabaster skin and that damn gorgeous tumble of messy hair. His beauty was in his energy, a little hard and guarded on the surface, but dynamic and captivating underneath. My mind drifted to the assortment of geodes Abby had arranged in her sprawling rock collection, the dark exteriors split open to reveal a glittering world of color. I shook my head at myself. No wonder I hadn't been on any dates. Here I was, sitting in silence and mentally comparing the guy I was with to a rock.

The waitress breezed by our table, delivering our beers and pinning us with a big grin. I gave Mikah's hand a squeeze, and he smiled shyly. "It sounds like your family cares a lot about you," I said belatedly. "They were cool with you being gay and all?"

Mikah snorted. "Yeah. My mom was totally awesome about it. Well, awesome but also kind of intense…. She works in the fashion industry, and she has a lot of queer friends. She kept having people over to, like, mentor me on gayness. My dad didn't care either way. Plus, Elena's queer too, and she was always super open about it. Weirdly, even though I knew they'd be cool with it, I was terrified to come out for some reason. The first person I told was my nonna, uh, my grandmother. She still lives in Sicily, but we're super close." His whole demeanor softened at the mention of his grandmother. "I wrote her this long-ass letter revealing that I was into guys. The angst was, truly, out of this world with teenage me. And even though she's like a total badass feminist who raised my dad and his sisters on her own, I was so worried. Right after I put the letter in the mail, I broke down and called her, which cost a fucking fortune because we ended up talking for, like, three hours. She was so great about it. She was just like, 'Your feelings are yours, caro. Be good to yourself and the ones you love. That's all you can do.' She's like a walking self-help book."

I grinned at his impression of his grandmother, his voice slipping into a soft, heavily accented register. Talking about his family seemed to relax Mikah.

"Sorry, I feel like I'm talking about myself a lot." Mikah rolled his eyes. "What about you?"

My body wanted to tense up, but I took a deep breath and relaxed my shoulders. I could focus on the present. The toddler at the table next to ours squealed with laughter as her big brother made silly faces. A gray-haired woman reached to adjust her companion's collar, clucking her tongue fondly. Soft, jazzy Christmas music emanated from the small radio on the shelf behind the bar. Mikah was looking at me expectantly, his hand still in mine.

"My parents never knew about me being gay, or anything. They died when I was in high school. Never got the chance to tell them."

"Matt...." Mikah's eyebrows drew together. "I don't know what to say. Shit. I'm so sorry."

Pressing my lips together, I gave a quick shake of my head. "Nah. It's fine." Mikah didn't look convinced. "But yeah, my brother has always been supportive. I didn't even have to come out. He mentioned, real casual, one afternoon that some girl was planning to ask me out. And he was like, 'But you aren't into girls, right?' I was so surprised I couldn't really deny it. Just warning you, if you meet him again, he's gonna be a huge pain in the ass. Ever since he saw...." I wasn't sure how to describe exactly what John had walked in on.

"Me dry humping you like my life depended on it?"

A laugh burst from me a little too loud, causing a few people to shoot amused looks in our direction. "Sure. But John's been relentless since. Dude's convinced you and I are soul mates or something." Heat bloomed on my cheeks. That had been a weird thing to admit. But Mikah gave me a soft smile as a comfortable silence settled between us. The waitress delivered our food, and I worried Mikah would actually spontaneously combust when she cheerfully commented that we looked good together. His blush was pretty damn endearing, though.

I devoured my chicken. It was delicious, with perfectly seasoned, crispy skin and tender dark meat. I existed in a state of perpetual hunger, so eating was definitely one of my favorite things to do. When I glanced at Mikah, his brown eyes were wide.

"What?" I asked, having to remind myself not to talk with my mouth full. Table manners were never a big priority in the Haskell household.

"You eat so fast!" Mikah's voice was high with surprise.

"And you're not eating at all." I gestured with my fork to his untouched plate of food.

"It's still superhot. Plus, I'm sure they're delicious, but these are *not* gnocchi." He narrowed his pretty eyes at the crisp dumplings like they might jump up and bite him.

I glanced at the menu written on a chalkboard next to the kitchen door. "It says Parisian…. So I guess they're French? I don't know much about food." I didn't want to admit that I had no earthly idea what gnocchi were, never mind what they were supposed to look like.

"Hmm." Mikah eyed his plate again before taking a bite. His eyes fluttered closed and he chewed slowly. My blood heated in my veins. "Okay, these are actually pretty fucking great. You want to try one?"

Food was the last thing on my mind at the moment, but I nodded. Mikah held out his fork to me, and when my eyes darted from the outstretched utensil to his face, his cheeks flushed. Had he wanted to feed me the bite of food?

"Um, here." Mikah stared down at the table as he rushed to hand me the fork. I tried real hard not to chuckle at how sweet he was.

Whatever it a gnocchi was, it tasted delicious: buttery crisp on the outside, light and fluffy inside. Really, though, all I wanted to taste was Mikah's mouth.

The front door of the restaurant banged open, frigid air and a swirl of snowflakes fluttering the heavy red curtain meant to keep out the cold. A loud group of skiers decked out in expensive coats bounded in laughing and, unfortunately, holding the door open for long enough that the temperature in the dining room probably dropped a good five degrees. The crisp wind was a relief on my lust-heated skin, but Mikah shivered. Without thinking I unzipped my hoodie and moved my chair around the table, draping my sweatshirt over his slim shoulders as I tucked my body in close to his. Moose perked up under the table at the commotion for a minute before snuffling back to sleep.

"Oh my God. Are you even real?" Mikah dropped his head on my shoulder as he spoke. My mouth curved up. We both got back to eating, me pulling my plate across the table to finish my last few bites of food while Mikah methodically enjoyed his. His movements were graceful, fluid. Close like this, I let myself watch the sharp bones of his jaw working as he chewed, his Adam's apple bobbing as he swallowed. Damn, why was watching him eat getting me hard? I glanced down at his throat again, noticing for the first time the gold chain around his neck. A small pinwheel symbol of a woman's face with three legs spiraling around it hung in the center. It was weirdly beautiful.

"What is that?" I gently grasped the pendant between two fingers.

Mikah glanced down at his chest. "Oh, it's the Trinacria. The symbol of Sicily. The head in the middle is supposed to be Medusa, and the three legs represent… something? My nonna explained it to me about a million times, but I always forget the specifics. But yeah, it used to belong to my grandfather. He died when my dad was a baby. My nonna gave it to me for my eighteenth birthday, and I've worn it ever sense." He lifted a shoulder, looking a little embarrassed.

"I like it," I said softly, momentarily giving in to the desire to trail my fingers up Mikah's throat to his jaw.

Mikah's lips fell open and he gasped softly. His eyes were heated as he set his fork down and cuddled in even closer. I wanted to cup my hand around the back of his neck and pull his mouth to mine. I had a feeling, though, that making out in the middle of a busy restaurant might not be the best idea. Jackson was undoubtedly the most liberal town in Wyoming, but it wasn't that liberal. So I settled with brushing my thumb over his lips and catching our server's eye to ask for the check.

As we stepped into the cold night air, fluffy snowflakes drifted around us, shimmering in the glow of the streetlight. Instinctively, I tipped my head back to look up at the sky. Nights out here never got old. Usually, the sky was so full of stars, it seemed more light than darkness. Tonight, though, a gray wash of clouds drifting and twisting in the wind obscured the display. Next to me Mikah fumbled with the zipper on his gigantic borrowed coat.

"Can I walk you to your car?" I bumped his shoulder with mine.

"How about I walk you to yours?" He offered me an impish grin, and my mouth stretched into a smile.

The smile grew impossibly wider as Mikah grasped my hand in his and tugged me in the direction of where I'd parked. Moose padded along behind us, pausing every few trees to sniff and dig at the snow.

For a small guy, Mikah was surprisingly strong as he pushed me against the door of my truck, slid his hands into my unzipped jacket, grabbed the back of my sweatshirt, and pulled me against him. The moment our lips connected, a sharp pang of lust twisted low in my stomach, and I groaned. Everything about Mikah made me melt, made me want things I knew I could never have. He licked into my mouth, as eager and giving as he'd been last time. The sound of his soft moans and the citrusy smell of his hair made me almost light-headed.

"God, I want you so bad." I was hyperaware of my racing heart, the buzzing tightness of my skin. Each touch felt electric.

"Me too," Mikah breathed, "but I should head home. Apparently everyone's waiting on me to decorate the tree." He rolled his eyes.

I smiled to hide my disappointment. "Okay. You want to get together again, though?"

Mikah tipped his face up to lock his eyes with mine for a long moment. "Why is this so easy with you?" His voice was soft, tentative.

Because I like you. Maybe too much. Because you give me something I need but didn't know I was missing. The words stayed inside. I bent to press a gentle, almost chaste kiss to Mikah's swollen lips.

"Get home safe," I murmured against his chilled skin. Dazed, I stood motionless among the whirling snow, watching until Mikah was swallowed by the dark.

Chapter Five

Mikah

THE morning was still, cracking with cold. Wrapping a threadbare cardigan over my sweatpants and T-shirt, I crept out of my bedroom. As an afterthought I tucked my worn copy of *One Hundred Years of Solitude* under my arm. It was a comfort book, and my night had, once again, been restless. I expected the typical morning commotion of my father's house: Elena sprawled on the buttery leather couch, half working and half watching the news; Luca and my father sipping coffee and droning on about clients and cases; Naomi flitting about in her fancy yoga clothes and making sure everyone had eaten enough breakfast. But the quiet of sleep blanketed the house. A glance at the ornate wooden clock over the mantle revealed it was not quite seven.

Drifting toward the illuminated Christmas tree—the tree from Matt's farm—now tastefully decorated with crystal icicles and silver ribbon, I wondered if Matt was awake yet. I liked imagining his calm, steady presence greeting the early risers purchasing last-minute Christmas trees. I pictured him moving through his morning: stretching in bed, muscles tensing as he pushed his body into the realm of wakefulness, stepping out into the sharp edge of a cold wind, his clear blue gaze drifting over the snow-dusted trees. The start of December meant Matt and his family were busier than ever selling Christmas trees and holiday greenery. He was so busy, in fact, that we'd only managed to get together a handful of times over the past two weeks for quick coffee dates and a series of kisses that left me so achy and distracted with desire, I was lucky I'd made the drive back into Jackson in one piece. It was probably for the best. There was no question that I was in way over my head.

Still, every moment we spent together felt precious. Whenever we were apart, Matt was all I could think about. The way his eyes locked on mine with an intensity that told me he was really listening to whatever I was saying. His adorably candid admission that, until we'd gotten dinner together, he'd never been on an actual date. The fact that just being in the same room as Matt rendered me overwhelmed with wanting. We'd texted a lot, and most nights we talked until I fell asleep on top of my phone. But I missed him. And I liked him. A lot. Too much.

My phone buzzed on the coffee table, jarring me from my increasingly dirty thoughts about what I'd like to do with Matt the next time we managed to get together. The sight of Matt's name on my phone's screen planted what I knew was a goofy grin on my face. I was glad everyone else was still asleep.

"Hey," I huffed out, trying to keep my voice even. I could be cool about this, even if I had answered the phone on the first ring.

"Hey." Matt's voice was low and soothing despite the roar of background noise.

"Where are you? It sounds like you're in a wind tunnel."

"Oh, uh, sorry. You're on speaker. I'm driving into Jackson, actually. For the market. It doesn't start till two, though. I was hoping you might want to hang out?"

Silently praying I managed to suppress the tiny squeal of delight at his words, I nodded. Then I realized he couldn't see me. "Yes. I mean, yeah. Totally. That sounds good. Do you want to meet for breakfast or something?" Okay, so I was kind of failing on the whole *be cool about this* front.

A smile was audible in Matt's voice as he rattled off the name and address of a bakery and ended the call a minute later with a promise to meet me there around nine.

After the world's fastest shower, spending way too much time deliberating over which sweater to wear, and suffering through an immobilizing storm of self-doubt over whether or not I would end up brokenhearted again, I was only about ten minutes late. I managed to find a parking spot right in front of the bakery, a little white house with black trim and window boxes bursting with sprigs of holly and glittery pinecones. Already there was a line out the door, but thanks to his height, I spotted Matt immediately in the crowd.

His eyes never left me as I trudged across the snowy sidewalk to meet him.

"Sorry I'm late. I, uh, got a little lost," I muttered the totally fake excuse, heart in my throat as Matt grinned and clapped me on the shoulder with an easy confidence I could never pull off. Was I supposed to give him a hug? Kiss him? Would he be okay with that in broad daylight on a crowded street? I knew my cheeks were flushed, but I hoped Matt would chalk my blush up to the cold and not to the heady mix of excitement and desire burning through me.

"Don't worry. There's plenty of time." His hand drifted from my shoulder to my face, fingers trailing the edge of my jaw and sifting into my hair. As always when I was with him, my doubts and fears evaporated. I hummed at the contact and leaned in close to him. We could totally forget this whole breakfast plan and make out in his truck if he wanted to.

Unfortunately for me, Matt actually wanted to eat breakfast, so we ended up crammed into a tiny corner table, sipping delicious coffee and tucking into giant plates of food. Or at least Matt ordered a giant breakfast. I'd opted for granola and almond milk, whereas Matt had ordered eggs, sausage, toast, and an extra side of sweet potato hash.

"Do you always do the farmer's market by yourself?" I asked, raising my voice over the din of excited tourists and the whirr of the coffee grinder.

Matt shook his head, swallowing a bite of toast. "No. John's gonna meet me over there later with the rest of the produce and eggs. I just—" His gaze dropped down to the table. "I just wanted to see you."

The goofy grin from earlier was back with a vengeance, and I rested my hand over his. "I wanted to see you too. Although I kind of wish we could hang out at your place instead." My tone was teasing, but I was dead serious. I loved spending any time I could with Matt, but I was pretty eager to get past the whole stealing-kisses-in-public phase of dating. Or hanging out. Whatever this was.

Matt shook his head, chuckling softly. "Me too. Wish things hadn't been so busy these past couple weeks. Maybe I can make you dinner? I'm not a great cook, but…." He trailed off with a shrug.

"Yes. Please." Once again I was probably overeager, but I didn't care. A whole night with Matt all to myself? I couldn't think of a better early Christmas present.

Clearly Matt was always a fast eater, because I'd barely taken two bites of my granola and he was nearly done with his enormous breakfast. He sat across the table, blue eyes trained intently on my face. A nervous laugh escaped my lips, and I set down my spoon, appetite for food completely gone.

"What's your favorite book?" As usual my mouth moved too quickly, and I blurted out the first random question my overwrought brain generated.

"*The Call of the Wild.* Probably read it about ten times."

The image of Matt's big body curled up on the couch as he reread a cherished book warmed me from the inside out. "Oh nice, Jack London, right? I loved that book when I was a kid. After that movie *Balto* came out, I was obsessed with sled dogs. Do you read a lot?"

Matt shrugged, looking both amused and a little embarrassed. "Yup. I read a lot of romance books, I guess." His eyes were fixed on his half-full coffee mug. If the idea of him reading animal adventure novels was adorable, it had nothing on the absurd cuteness of this giant of a man reading romance.

"Jesus Christ… seriously, how are you even real?" I beamed at him before I reined myself in. "I haven't read much romance, but Elena's a big fan. She reads all this queer romantic sci-fi stuff. What kind do you usually read?"

Matt rubbed the back of his neck. "Don't know… gay ones. I don't meet a lot of beautiful guys like you. Have to make do with the next best thing."

Heat crept up from my collar into my cheeks, and suddenly the whine of the espresso machine and the jingling Christmas music faded away. The need to touch Matt, to wrap my arms around his thick torso and rub my face against the fabric of his flannel shirt, overwhelmed me. I squeezed my eyes shut.

Rough fingers brushed over mine on the table, and Matt smiled his small, almost shy smile. "Want to take a walk? There's a bookstore around the corner. I have an hour or so before I need to set up at the market."

"My dad's place isn't far." My voice sounded needy even to my own ears, but I forged ahead. "You could come over and we could… hang out for a little bit."

Matt drained his coffee cup and looked at me for a long moment. The heat of his gaze reminded me suddenly of my first kiss. Walking home from school on a crisp New York autumn day, the sweet smells of wet leaves and roasted nuts mingling with car exhaust. Truman Miller, my best friend, had glanced at me again and again as we walked close, arms brushing. Outside my building, for all the doormen and ladies in fur coats waiting for taxis to see, he kissed me. Now, just like it did then, the air thickened and crackled with energy. A hot hunger rocketed through my veins, but I somehow knew what Matt was going to say before he even shook his head.

"Mikah." Matt's voice was pitched so low, I had to lean forward. His clean pine smell pulled me even closer. "When we do that"—he bumped his knee against mine under the table and I shivered—"I'm not rushing it, okay? I want to take my time."

I nodded, a little dazed at the thought of Matt taking sex so seriously. I didn't know what to do with his intensity. It was both thrilling and terrifying. He was so unlike anyone I'd dated in the past. So honest that I felt I needed to be honest in return.

I floated out of the restaurant, clumsy with desire. The snap of cold against my skin did little to distract me. The sky was sharply blue, the sun glimmering off the snow. My boots slipped on the icy sidewalk as we walked the few blocks to the bookstore, and Matt steadied me, letting go of my shoulder far too quickly. I wanted nothing more than to hold Matt's hand, to stake a public claim on this man in the middle of the sun-drenched sidewalk teeming with holiday shoppers. It felt silly, childish even. We'd already made out a handful of times and had just been vaguely discussing when we would finally have sex. I could grab his hand on the sidewalk, for fuck's sake. All around us couples darted in and out of Western-themed tourist stores, laughing and holding hands without a second thought. Already exhausted with my fretting, I pushed down the butterflies in my stomach, reached forward, and slipped my hand into his. He smiled and laced our fingers together, tucking me in close against him as we made our way along the snowy street.

I've always loved losing myself in independent bookstores, and Jackson's didn't disappoint. Cozy and thoughtfully laid out, the store was packed with boisterous families, sulky teens, and couples clearly on romantic holiday vacations. Salt spots and snowy footprints dotted the gray wooden floors, and a cheerful older lady in a Santa hat greeted us as we pulled the door closed behind us. Matt let go of my hand as we crossed the threshold into the shop and immediately navigated over to a display of cookbooks. Extinguishing the small flare of disappointment in my chest at the loss of contact, I drifted over to the somewhat secluded, very deserted poetry section. The selection of titles was impressive, well curated, and eclectic. I lost all sense of time as I sank into a collection of poems by local Wyoming authors. Then the weight of strong arms winding around my shoulders from behind startled me back into the present. A smile glowed on my face as Matt pulled me against him.

"Sorry. I saw a cookbook I'd been thinking of ordering for my sister-in-law. Glad I didn't, though. It had about ten recipes for fancy roasted chicken. And half of them had fruit. She hates fruit in savory dishes." He pressed his lips against the top of my head, and warmth seeped down my entire body.

I laughed at this weirdly specific gripe and turned to face him, giving in to my desire to burrow my face into the soft flannel of his shirt. The fabric smelled as good as I remembered, like pine and clean laundry. For a long moment we stayed wrapped up in each other. Then Matt's phone buzzed in his pocket, and he groaned as he looked at the screen.

"Sorry. I gotta go."

"Is everything okay?" I hoped I didn't sound as disappointed as I felt.

Matt chuckled and rolled his eyes fondly. "Yeah. John decided to bring some extra wreaths and stuff to sell at the market, but we don't have room. So he wants to sell in the parking lot." He shook his head, a few short strands of blond hair falling across his forehead.

I reached up to smooth them back and ghosted my lips over the side of his mouth. His face was rough with stubble, and his breath caught in his throat.

"Mikah," he sighed against my skin, "I can't wait to see you again." He kissed me fast and hard. Then, with a promise to call me after the market, he was gone.

CHRISTMAS was a few days away and, much to my selfish chagrin, Matt's farm was once again flooded with customers. His sister-in-law put up additional flyers around town to advertise the trees, and as a result, the farm had been busy from early morning until well past sundown. So dinner at Matt's cabin never worked out. In fact, we were back to lots of texting, calls, and occasional dates that ended far too soon and involved far too much clothing and far too little alone time. Matt was always on my mind. Every time he touched me, all of my nerve endings lit up like the Christmas tree we bought from him. My need for Matt was unlike anything I'd experienced with other men. I craved his presence, was stunned by his unique ability to turn me on and calm me down at the same time. Thankfully, though, I had devised a plan so the two of us could spend more than a few stolen hours together.

Today my morning routine played out as usual: burn my mouth trying to guzzle too-hot coffee, nibble a Nutella-slathered slice of toast, scroll through email. The sight of a familiar name in my inbox lodged a lump in my throat, leaving me breathless. *Jordan Goode.* I laughed fondly at the email's subject line: *Happy Non-Denominational Winter Holiday!* Reading my former student's words brought an enormous grin to my face.

> *Hey Mr. C!*
>
> *I was gonna start this email with a holiday greeting but I have some pretty awesome news, tbh. I won the gold medal award in the MassArts competition you told me to enter! I ended up using the poem you and Ms. Fernandez helped revise, the one about the boy at my dad's barbershop. My mom cried at the ceremony, which was actually embarrassing as hell. But you were right, she's totally cool with the whole gay thing. She's all proud of me for being a legit poet.*
>
> *Now I'll be polite and wish you a Merry Christmas. Idk if you're already teaching at a new school or what, but we miss you and wish you could come back. Fernandez and Lasky both got lunch duty and none of the other teachers let us eat in their rooms, so now me and Santi have to suffer in the cafeteria. I swear my eardrums are gonna burst if I have to spend another period in there.*
>
> *Anyway, I know this is cheesy as fuck (you're not my teacher anymore so I can swear!) but I just wanted to thank you. For everything. You*

*actually made writing fun and it's
stupid that we don't have creative
writing anymore bc it was totally
everyone's favorite class. So thanks,
dude. You'll be hearing from me
soon when I start begging for college
letters of rec.*
    —Jordan

At the outset of my second year teaching, I had immediately, wrongly, labeled Jordan as a difficult student. Strolling into class late, if he showed up at all, he'd rolled his eyes through my carefully prepared lectures and scoffed at my terrible puns and dad jokes. He mocked everything from my clothes to the framed picture of my family on my desk. He didn't like me, and I was frustrated by my inability to connect with him. Then I read his writing. Vivid prose that transported me to his chaotic, loving home in Jamaica Plain. Poetry that brimmed with such striking, fresh imagery, it always made me pause and reread with held breath. The boy had a gift. So I was honest with him: told him his attitude sucked but his words were profound, that he was too smart to waste class time staring at his phone. And for some reason, he listened. He brought in a spiral notebook full of intensely beautiful work and asked for my feedback.

"Texting your man?" Elena's voice pulled my attention from the effusive, likely embarrassingly sappy email I was tapping out in response to Jordan.

"No. Emailing a student. Well, former student. He sent me the nicest email!" Excitement hitched in my voice as I showed my sister the message.

"Aw, look at you having an impact on youth." Elena helped herself to a large gulp of my coffee. "You must be psyched about the Walton interview."

I was not. Rationally I knew as a teacher with only two years of experience, I was incredibly fortunate to even be considered for an interview at the elite Manhattan prep school my siblings and I had attended. A large portion of the Walton School's faculty had doctorates. Many taught at Ivy League universities prior to gracing the classrooms of the Upper East Side campus. Although I'd excelled academically at Walton and stayed in touch with a few of my favorite teachers, I wasn't exactly a notable alum. I'd followed in my father's and Luca's footsteps, applying and getting accepted to Harvard. Unlike the other Cerullo men, though, I'd focused my studies on literature and creative writing. My dad and Luca went on to law school. I got a master's in education.

A few weeks after Boston Public Schools made the announcement that they planned to eliminate over a hundred teachers, I'd gotten an email from Dr. Yang, my ninth-grade English teacher and all-around inspirational hero. Dr. Yang had captivated me while I cowered in the back row of her classroom, thrilled by the material but too terrified to raise my hand and participate. She gave me books by Octavia Butler and introduced me to the work of Frank O'Hara, to this day my absolute favorite poet. She showed me, although in my blood I already knew, that it was okay to be queer.

Now, as the newly named head of the Humanities Department, Dr. Yang invited me to interview for an open position teaching creative writing at Walton. Reading between the lines of her email, it was clear the position was mine for the taking. On paper the job was ideal: prestigious, well-paid, and promising the kind of pedagogical freedom I'd never had in public schools. But I wanted nothing more than to go back to my old job: finding ways to engage students who hadn't grown up with a team of tutors to help them with every paper, bolstering the school's gay-straight alliance, and organizing very laughable but weirdly fun poetry slams.

"*Tutto bene*?" Elena waved her hand in front of my face, concern rippling over her features.

"Yeah, I'm fine." I shivered, my awareness returning to the present. The kitchen was cold. Peering at the towering stone fireplace that served as the centerpiece of the house, I found the hearth dark and empty. When I'd arrived back in November, my father had demonstrated how to build and effectively light a fire. Although it seemed straightforward enough, it clearly wasn't my strong suit. Now, as I stacked dry logs and crumpled newspaper, I heard the distinct sound of my father's leather slippers shuffling across the knotty pine floors. No time like the present to put my plan into motion.

"*Faccio io.*" My father gave my shoulders an affectionate squeeze and squatted down next to me in front of the fireplace and took over without my asking. Although his face still bore a few lines from his pillow, he was, as always, neatly composed. His navy blue pajamas, undoubtedly Egyptian cotton, were devoid of wrinkles, and he smelled of the expensive woodsy cologne he always wore. The lenses of his stylish tortoiseshell glasses were never smudged, his close-cropped salt-and-pepper beard never unkempt. My father had grown up poor, my nonna struggling to feed four children and pay the rent on their Palermo apartment on her teacher's salary. Now, my father wasn't shy about basking in the financial success of his law firm. His standards were high. *Anything worth doing is worth doing right.* I bet he'd said those words a thousand times.

"I could have done it," I grumbled, but before the words even escaped my lips, my father had a fire blazing in the hearth. Chuckling, my dad pressed a kiss to the side of my head and stood, dusting his hands off briskly.

"Are you and Elena cooking today? I have a call at nine. But afterward I can help."

I snorted out a laugh at my father's offer. He was, indisputably, a horrible cook. He'd never learned growing up, simply letting his mother and sisters stuff him full of their delicious caponata and homemade bread. His attention had been fixed solely on school and earning money. Now, anytime he tried to cook, he was too easily distracted by email or work calls to make it through a recipe.

"Yup!" Elena called from the kitchen, her voice rising over the sound of grinding coffee beans. "We're going to the store when it opens. But I'm kinda worried about finding the right stuff. I mean, do they even sell baccalà out here?"

"I called ahead to order it," I replied, trying and failing not to sound smug. Worried we wouldn't be able to purchase the ingredients for the seafood-heavy Christmas Eve meal we always prepared, I special-ordered most of the produce and fish ahead. Then, distracted by a certain hot blond farmer, I promptly forgot to share this information with Elena.

"Smart boy." My dad grinned at me. Then he pulled out his phone. I knew I had to ask him now or risk losing him down the email rabbit hole. My stomach clenched. I hadn't even asked Matt about this yet. He probably had plans with his brother.

"Is it cool if I invite someone over for Christmas Eve dinner?" The words tumbled out so quickly, my dad actually looked up from his phone.

"Sorry, what?" he asked, stowing his phone in his bathrobe pocket.

Articulating the words slowly and clearly, I repeated myself, this time in Italian. I bumped my forehead with my fist. Maybe my grand plan was stupid. Would Matt even want to spend the holiday with some random guy he'd only known for a few weeks?

"The man you've been seeing?" He and Luca could have been identical twins rather than father and son in that moment: same squaring of the shoulders, same assessing gaze, same slight quirk of the lips.

"Yes. Matt. Honestly, I'm making the whole damn meal, so I don't even know why I checked with you." My dad's dark eyebrows soared toward his bald head. A sigh escaped my lips. "Well, okay, it's your house, so...."

He smiled fondly. "Mikah, of course he's welcome. Naomi will be thrilled. I can't wait to meet him." He was being charming now, aware that his paternal protectiveness had irked me.

The moment our father wandered off to his office, Elena's strong fingers closed around my bicep, and she yanked me into the kitchen. Our nonna's recipe cards were scattered over the marble countertop.

Elena clapped her hands together in the kind of let's-get-pumped gesture I remembered from her days of field hockey and competitive swimming. "So you *like* him." Her eyes were lighter than mine, more whiskey than coffee, and the golden flecks caught in the crystalline morning light.

I felt my face tighten, and I made a noncommittal noise in the back of my throat. "What about you? Are you still seeing Sylvie?"

"Pretty sneaky, bro. Deflection isn't going to work this time. And no. Anyway, I know that's Mikah for 'yes, I really like him but I'm pretending I don't give a shit,' right?" My sister saw right through my mask of indifference to the writhing tangle of desires and worries within.

"I guess." I couldn't look at her, so I pulled open the gleaming professional-grade refrigerator. As I stared at the neat arrangements of mineral water, cheese wrapped in brown paper, and Naomi's green juices, Matt was all I saw. His angular jaw, the soft curve of his upper lip, the sweep of wheat-colored hair. Somehow, simply picturing his face slowed my pulse.

"This again?" I turned to find an expression of genuine exasperation on my sister's face. "Look, I'm not going to act like Dad and Luca. You're a grown-ass man who can figure out his own life. But I hate that you overthink shit so much that you never let yourself enjoy anything. You're always so sure it's all going to be a disaster, so you shut down before anything happens. When your school laid you off, you were totally convinced your teaching career was over, and now you're interviewing at one of the best schools in the country. So, chill, okay? I know you had a rough year. But not every guy is going to be like Josh. Besides, it's nothing but a holiday fling, right? You know you're allowed to have fun." Elena twirled a lock of chestnut hair around her finger. "Just try to let yourself be happy, okay?"

I felt the truth of her words on every inch of my skin. But if I handed Matt even a shard of myself, the barest sliver, I knew I would crumble into him. And I wasn't sure I would want to rebuild myself again.

Chapter Six

Matt

THE flowers were a mistake. My grip tightened around the cellophane-wrapped bouquet of daisies I'd picked up at the supermarket. Daisies had always been my mother's favorite. She had a tattoo of them on her upper arm, and when I was little, I'd loved tracing my fingers over the fading yellow and white. Now, anytime I saw them growing wild in fields or behind the glass case of the grocery store flower section, I thought of her.

Through the two narrow windows flanking the imposing wooden door, I glimpsed an elegant floral display in the foyer. Even through the frosty glass it was obvious the arrangement was professional: sprays of white calla lilies and hydrangeas, sharp sprigs of holly with taut red berries, boughs of pine, and spindles of eucalyptus. I wanted to throw my flowers back in my truck and jump in after them. Everything about the Cerullos' enormous house intimidated me: the way the golden light from the windows reflected off the iced-over surface of the adjacent pond, the towering stone chimney pouring smoke into the indigo sky, the beautiful craftsmanship of the rustic wood exterior. Pulling a deep breath through my nose, I rang the doorbell. This would be okay. Mikah was inside. He had invited me to spend Christmas Eve with him. I was wanted here.

Usually I spent the holidays alone. For a few years after my brother married Katie, I'd piled into John's truck with the two of them to visit Katie's parents on the Flathead Reservation in Montana. Katie's family was nothing but welcoming, clapping me on the back and ruffling my hair good-naturedly the moment I stepped over the threshold of their house. They were great, but I still felt out of place around the huge, boisterous family that wasn't mine. So I rekindled the tradition of stove-top stuffing and *It's a Wonderful Life*, this time without John's colorful commentary. I didn't mind spending the holidays with only Moose's snores and Elvis's music for company.

When Mikah had shown up at the farm two days ago right in the middle of a rush of harried last-minute tree buyers, I hadn't hesitated to pull him behind the barn and kiss him senseless as the snow drifted around us and the line at the register piled up. When we'd finally parted, breathless and unable to hide our grins, Mikah had asked me to join his family for their traditional Italian Christmas Eve meal. He'd gotten flustered, blushing hotly and fumbling over his words. I said yes so quickly, we both dissolved into laughter.

This morning I'd been fidgety with excitement as I ironed the wrinkles out of my favorite green flannel shirt. I actually whistled as I oiled my nicer pair of boots. And when I came back from town last night with the flowers and a large paper bag from the outdoor supply store, John and Katie had exchanged a look that heated the tips of my ears.

I had not, however, expected to pull up to an actual mansion when I followed my phone's GPS to the address Mikah gave me. Although Mikah had mentioned his father being a lawyer, I'd somehow assumed his family's home would be modest. Nice, maybe one of the older houses on the outskirts of town, well cared for but nothing fancy. This place was definitely fancy. As I looked once again at the Cerullos' house, my eyebrows knit together. If Mikah's family was this wealthy, why did he drive such a beat-up car? Why did he wear nothing but torn-up jeans and tattered sweaters? Did he like slumming it? Was that why he liked me? Fire tore through me, a mix of shame and hurt. Then Mikah pulled the door open, and his soft smile was a splash of cool water.

"Hi." He laughed nervously and gestured for me to come in.

I didn't know where to look first. Both Mikah and the interior of the house were astonishing in their beauty. Both surprised me with their bright cheer. It was the first time I'd seen Mikah wearing anything colorful. His garnet sweater somehow made his creamy skin and dark hair glow warmer than usual.

"These are for you," I mumbled, thrusting the flowers at him. Looking around, though, it was abundantly clear that the daisies would probably just end up in the garbage. There were, in addition to the huge arrangement I'd spied through the door, flowers and holiday arrangements everywhere. A garland of pine and white lights twined around the rough-hewn banister. Large pots of poinsettias flanked the archway into the kitchen. There were even swags of juniper adorning the wrought-iron chandelier.

Mikah startled me by pressing a soft kiss to the corner of my mouth. "Thank you, I love daisies. Here, come on in, and I'll put them in some water."

The kitchen was loud. Over the roar of the vent fan above the stove and the classical music tinkling from a built-in sound system, every member of the Cerullo family seemed to be speaking at once. As I followed Mikah into the room, however, they all stopped. And they all turned to look at me.

"Um, so this is Matt." Mikah gave my forearm a quick, reassuring squeeze. "Matt, this is… my entire family."

Elena waved enthusiastically at me, offering me a smile so kind and genuine, my breath came easier.

"Thanks for having me." My voice was low and rough. I reached into the shopping bag for the apple butter and huckleberry preserves I'd put up last fall. The small mason jars with their handmade labels looked out of place in the state-of-the-art kitchen. "I brought you these."

"Thank you so much. How thoughtful!" A slim woman with glossy black hair and lots of silver jewelry stepped forward to pull me into a perfumed hug. "I'm Naomi, Mikah's stepmom. I'm so happy you're here! It'll be nice to have another person in the house who doesn't lapse into Italian during every conversation." Her laugh and glance at the man I guessed was Mikah's dad were a little self-conscious.

"Matt, it's a pleasure. I'm Stefano." Mikah's father shook my hand, his grip firm but not over-the-top. When Luca grasped my hand, however, I had to wonder if he was trying to break it. It was funny to see how much Mikah's older brother resembled their father, both of them tall and broad, with dignified faces and bronze skin. I figured Mikah and Elena must have taken after their mother. They were both graceful and slim, with a kind of delicate wildness that reminded me of the foxes I saw stalking quietly through the woods sometimes: dark eyes, quick movements, guarded intelligence. They both had heavy, serious eyebrows, messy hair, and pale skin. And they definitely shared the exact same snarky grin.

"So what can I get you to drink?" Naomi asked with the poised air of a perfect hostess. "There's a bit of champagne left in the fridge, some of the Etna Bianco I think too? Or if you'd like red, Luca can run down to the cellar."

"I'm okay for now, thank you."

"If you are worried about driving, don't be. You are more than welcome to spend the night. We are not prudes in this house," Mikah's father stated matter-of-factly, his voice heavily accented.

"Jesus, Dad!" Mikah turned from the stove where he'd been checking a bubbling pot. Our eyes met across the room, and my heart jolted in my chest. I'm sure we both blushed like teenagers.

Next to him Elena snorted. "Okay, food will be ready in, like, ten minutes. We can all stop embarrassing Mikah until we're at the dinner table." She winked at me.

When I slid into a chair next to Mikah around the wide, tree-slab dining table, my mouth automatically curved into a smile. Although he'd been dashing around, putting the finishing touches on the elaborate meal, Mikah had taken the time to arrange the daisies in a vase, placing them in the middle of a cluster of red and gold candles at the center of the table. When he noticed me looking at them, he reached for my hand and didn't let go.

"*Allora*, before we eat, I propose a toast." Mikah's father stood, brushing nonexistent lint from his blazer. He began speaking in rapid-fire Italian, and Naomi caught my eye, shooting me a look that said *told you.* I pressed my lips together to hide my smile.

"What did he say?" I whispered in Mikah's ear after we'd clinked glasses and sipped our champagne. Or, prosecco, Mikah told me. I'd never had it before, but I liked the soft fizziness in my mouth.

"Oh, just a bunch of stuff about family and new beginnings and how lucky he is. He gets way too sentimental this time of year." Mikah rolled his eyes, but I could tell his heart wasn't really in the gesture. Then his eyes widened, and his expression shifted from snarky to panicked. "Wait, do you like seafood?" He glanced at the sideboard, crowded with numerous platters under silver domes.

I shrugged. "I like trout and salmon. Haven't tried much else."

Mikah bit his lip and want flashed through me. "Okay, well, if you'd like, I can make you a plate?" His sheepish expression morphed my want into need. I was desperate to pull him into my lap, to wrap my arms around him, to drag the tip of my nose along the warm skin of his neck.

"Sure." I nodded easily.

"Don't worry at all if you don't like something." Mikah was still holding my hand, and I was reluctant to let him go as he stood.

He returned a moment later with a plate full of unfamiliar food. I couldn't help but eye it skeptically. I recognized spaghetti, lightly coated in tomato sauce and studded with olives. There were fried things and a thick slice of bread smeared with white and dusted with flecks of parsley. There was also something that looked horrifyingly tentacled. I took a giant gulp of champagne.

Mikah tipped his head back in a bright laugh. "You look pretty freaked-out." When he grasped my hand again, I relaxed.

"Nah." I glanced around the table. Naomi and Stefano were still serving themselves while Elena and Luca were caught up in an argument about which wine would be best to serve first. "Just, uh, what is all this?"

Again Mikah grinned. It was nice to see him so relaxed. "So, it's the Festa dei Sette Pesci. Most Italians, the Catholic ones anyway, don't eat meat on Christmas Eve, so we do a big seafood meal." He pointed down at the spaghetti on my plate. "That's pasta puttanesca; it's a little spicy but really good if you like anchovies." He raised his eyebrows as if waiting for a response.

"Never had 'em," I murmured.

"I think you'll like it. Next to that is bread with baccalà mantecato. It's a salt cod spread. We're kinda flexible with what we serve every year, but I always make this." Mikah fake-preened. "It's kind of my specialty. Anyway, let's see. I gave you a little bit of fried calamari and smelts. Make sure you squeeze the lemon over them. And, um, in the middle, that's sea bass. Oh, and insalata di mare. Basically, it's a whole bunch of shellfish and octopus."

As strange as the food was, it was undeniably delicious. I was aware of Mikah watching me eat, so I paused and set down my fork. Damn, I ate way faster than anyone in his family. "You made all this?" I asked.

"No! He so did not!" Elena cut in, all mock-indignant. "I made the sea bass and the salad."

"Yeah, the two easiest dishes." Mikah waved a piece of octopus speared on his fork.

"Oh, okay, so who spent two hours making the cannoli, then?" Elena had perfected the art of the arched eyebrow.

"Fair enough." Mikah laughed.

I returned to eating, willing myself to chew slowly and actually savor the balanced flavors of garlic, lemon, and herbs. Around me the conversation flowed in undulating waves of Italian and English. But even if I'd understood every word, I still would have been at sea. There were snippets about the upcoming opera season in New York. Mikah and his father argued about a poet I'd never heard of. Elena and Luca resumed their conversation about wine. I liked the way they talked, interrupting each other and filling in the ends of sentences, a soft thrum of genuine care underlying every word and gesture. This was certainly nothing like the meals I'd grown up with. Before I knew it, I'd cleaned my plate.

"Matt!" Mika's father's voice rang out over the din of conversation. My head snapped up. "You need more food. What can I get you?"

Patting my stomach, I declined. "I'm pretty full, thanks, Mr. Cerullo."

"Stefano," he corrected with a very Mikah-like grin, "and nonsense. You want some more fish, or perhaps some calamari?"

Knowing I wasn't about to win this argument, I asked for more of the baccalà, although I forgot the word and had to communicate by pointing to Mikah's still mostly full plate. As I started in on my second helping of food, Luca's gaze rested on me.

"So, Matt, Mikah told me you're a farmer?" Luca's voice was perfectly neutral. I didn't know what kind of law he practiced, but I knew I would hate having to face the guy in a courtroom. I always found it difficult to talk to people like him, people with unreadable expressions whose every word seemed calculated to produce a specific effect.

"Yup." I nodded once, unsure of what else to say. I dragged my finger through the condensation on my glass of fizzy water.

"How'd you get into that? Seems like a tough business."

"My brother and I inherited the land after our parents passed." No point in beating around the bush. "Now we're certified organic and doing pretty well. I like the work."

"What made you decide to go the organic route?" Luca sounded genuinely interested now, so I answered honestly.

"My folks didn't really lead the healthiest lifestyle. Didn't take great care of the land. My dad just dumped chemicals on the crops and hoped for the best. The yields were low, and we struggled to make it. My brother, John, was real into 4-H. Knew a lot about actual growing practices and stuff. Honestly, the profit margins are better for organics if you're a small farm like us. The certification was real expensive, but it means we have a wider appeal to a lot of the restaurants and markets in Jackson. Chefs go pretty wild for fancy vegetables, I guess. And I make a lot of value-added products for us too. Pickles, jams, that kind of thing."

Truthfully the decision to overhaul the farm had been all John's. After my parents died, I stuttered to a halt. I quit football, quit school, quit doing anything. But John had been solid. He was single-minded in his dedication to care for me and the land. When I woke up from my shock, I found the fields cleared, the house cleaned up, the rusted-out cars gone from the driveway. I was proud of the business we'd built and grateful for my brother.

Mikah twined his fingers with mine, as if he sensed my slight discomfort. "Okay." He shot his brother a pointed glare. "You can stop interrogating him now."

Luca laughed easily, a surprising, hearty sound from such a refined-looking guy. "Fine. You seem like a good dude, Matt. I'm glad Mikah invited you."

AS we settled on the floor in front of the massive stone fireplace, Mikah nuzzled into my side, his head resting on my shoulder. It was nice, sitting together in comfortable quiet, sipping strong coffee and listening to the crackle of the flames. Through the huge windows, I noticed that the snow had stopped, and the moon glazed the landscape in an opalescent glow. Inside everything was warm and peaceful. I couldn't help looking again and again at the spruce in the corner, surrounded by silver-wrapped gifts and decorated so elegantly, it looked straight out of a design magazine. It had been a long time since I'd felt this good.

After insisting on cleaning up the dishes, I'd been once again stuffed with more food than I could ever eat. And I loved eating. This time it was Elena, plying me with cannoli and some kind of delicious honey-coated fritters. Having tried more new foods in a single day than I had in the rest of my adult life, I was impressed with Mikah's and Elena's cooking abilities. Once we were comfortably situated in the living room with our desserts and coffee, Mikah told me excitedly about learning to cook with his grandmother. This year, for the first time, she'd stayed in Italy for the holidays, and Mikah's disappointment was etched into his features. Again, I was struck by how close-knit his family was.

"Actually"—Mikah sat up, shaking off his sleepy haze—"should we skype Nonna? I think it's morning in Palermo, right?"

Mikah's dad glanced down at his gold watch and made a face. "Eh, it's early."

Elena laughed. "She's awake. She probably got up at, like, three to start making the timballo. I'll grab my computer, and we can see if she's online."

A moment later Elena slid on socked feet back into the living room, a ringing sound emanating from her laptop.

Everyone aside from me and Naomi crammed together on the toffee-colored leather couch. Wondering if I should excuse myself to text John, I stayed seated by the fireplace. My brother and his family were probably headed back from Montana now, making the nearly seven-hour drive so Abby could wake up and open presents at home on Christmas morning. Abby would be passed out in the back seat; Katie would be buzzing with excitement to lay out gifts and eat the cookies her daughter made for Santa. I didn't know if Mikah would actually want me to spend the night, but if he did, I could ask John to take Moose. Abby would be thrilled. I had a nagging suspicion that one day I would come back from the market only to find that my niece had kidnapped my dog.

Vaguely I was aware of another voice, spunky and heavily accented, mixing with the others. But it was only when Mikah lobbed a throw pillow at my head that I realized that his grandmother was asking to meet me. My stomach dropped. Why did this feel like such a big deal? When I stepped behind the couch, Mikah twisted to look up at me, his eyes so soft, I wanted to bend and kiss him. Instead I rested my hand on his bony shoulder, peering down at the woman on the screen. She was one of those older women whose age was hard to pin down. Her gray hair was pulled back into a smooth bun, and she had laugh lines around her mouth. Her dark eyes glimmered with humor.

"*Buon Natale,* Matt!" She waved at me from the small screen. I lifted my hand in a greeting, feeling surprised at my own nervousness. "So you are Mikah's new boyfriend? Very handsome."

Mikah waved his hands frantically. "Nonna!" He shot me an apologetic glance over his shoulder.

My heart raced at her use of the word. Imagining Mikah as my boyfriend, sharing meals, waking up in bed with him in my arms, building a life together, flooded me with warm, bright joy.

"Has Mikah played the piano for you?" Her question lifted my attention from the screen to the upright piano tucked in the corner. The top was decorated with framed photos and potted plants. I'd noticed the instrument earlier, but I'd been more interested in the pictures: the three siblings posing goofily on a beach, Luca looking serious in a cap and gown, Elena beaming next to what looked like a homemade robot, teenage Mikah scowling in field full of sunflowers.

"No, ma'am." I massaged Mikah's shoulders, trying to signal that he didn't have to play if he didn't want to. His family, though, had other ideas.

"Yes, I love it!" Naomi, who was standing next to me, spoke for the first time since the start of the call. "Please, Mikah, play something. I've never heard you either."

"Do the 'Waltz of the Flowers.' We missed *The Nutcracker* this year. And I heard the NYC Ballet has been killing it since Asha Shadid took over as director." Elena was bouncing in her seat at the idea. "For God's sake, Mikah, we're culture starved out here in the Wild West."

Mikah grumbled but rose to his feet, shuffling over to take a seat on the small piano bench. His father followed him, holding up the laptop so his grandmother could watch. Something in Mikah transformed as he aligned his slim fingers on the black and white keys. His focus intensified, like everything else in the room melted away. Then he started to play, each motion precise and measured as he filled the room with beauty. I couldn't take my eyes off him, his plush lips pressed into a firm line, his straight eyebrows pushed together. He was playing from memory, as if the notes were flowing directly from his mind to the piano. Too soon, Mikah finished, pushing his hair back and shooting me a shy smile. Then he was in my arms, and I realized I'd pulled him into a tight hug there in front of his entire family to see.

I pressed my mouth to his ear, my voice dry and brittle as sandpaper as I thanked him in a low whisper. The same bright warmth flushed through my chest. He'd given me so much tonight, I wasn't quite sure what I was thanking him for.

Chapter Seven

Mikah

I'VE always loved the sound of snow crunching underfoot. When I lived in Cambridge, sometimes I would get up early after a big nor'easter and tromp out into the cold-quiet streets. Walking alone I'd relished the squeaks and cracks of ice and snow sliding off branches and settling onto the ground. I would watch the poststorm clouds churning in the sky, softly outlined in gold as the sun made its ascent. The cold out here was different, sharper and cleaner, glinting like a knife. The wind exhaled a swirl of snow, and I pulled my jacket close around my body. Luca's coat was way too big to wear, so I was suffering in my flimsy denim jacket. Next to me, Matt was quiet save for his heavy footfalls. He hadn't said anything when I suggested we go for a walk, just gave me one of his quiet nods and went to retrieve his coat.

I pulled in breaths of cold, dry air, savoring its snap at the back of my throat before exhaling clouds of steam. Idly I wondered why that was always so satisfying. When I looked up, the sky was clear and awash with stars, so many it looked almost dusty.

"Is that the Milky Way?" I asked Matt, gesturing upward.

"Yup." Another silent nod. "You can see the northern lights sometimes too."

We'd walked halfway around the pond, a good distance away from the house. My eyes had adjusted to the dark, taking in the white glow of the moon against the snow. Why was Matt being so quiet? Had my family overwhelmed him with their interrogations and boyfriend talk? Did he want to leave? Maybe it was better if he did. If he wasn't into me, I'd rather find out now instead of after I'd already made a fool of myself. Now that we were outdoors, he seemed calmer but still thoughtful, hands stuffed into the pockets of his work coat, eyes cast upward at the night sky.

"Sorry if my family was a little intense," I mumbled, feeling a bit like I was interrupting his thinking.

Matt stopped walking. "I liked them," he said after a long moment of looking at me. "I liked them a lot." Something shifted in his expression then, going from pensive to relaxed. "All the Italian was a little intimidating, and they're definitely pretty... sophisticated."

I chuckled. "I guess so. I told my dad to stick to English, but he forgets when he's home."

Matt just shrugged, no big deal. He was still staring at me. I wanted to close the distance between us, but it seemed like he still had something to say. So I waited.

Finally, when he asked the question, it surprised me. "Why do you like me?" Matt's eyes immediately snapped from my face back up to the stars, as if he was preemptively nervous about my response and couldn't watch while I said something that might hurt him.

I reached for his face, cupping his cold cheek gently and pulling his attention back to me. That seemed to make him happy, his lips twitching up at the corners. Mine followed suit. Everything about Matt was wholesome, like biting into an oven-warm slice of bread, hearty and good and nourishing. His earnestness deserved an honest response, not my reflex default to sarcasm in the face of scary emotions.

"Well, for one you're insanely hot," I teased. Shit. It came out too flippant, and Matt's expression shuttered. I hurried on, stumbling hard over my words. "And you… you make me feel calm, I guess. Like it's actually kind of wild. I mean, I can be kind of, I don't know, uptight sometimes. But I just really like being with you." My face was probably glowing in the dark, it was so hot.

Matt drew me to him, wrapping me up in his unzipped coat as he pressed a kiss to the top of my head. When he spoke, his words were muffled by my hair. "So you're not, uh, slumming it with me or something?" The note of apprehension in his voice broke my heart.

My head snapped up so fast my neck cracked. "No!" I was horrified by the notion that Matt had even worried about that. My panic pushed a tangle of words out of me. "Not at all. Shit. I'm so sorry if I did anything to make you feel like that…." I dragged a hand over my face. This was so hard to talk about. "I like spending time with you because you're sweet and weirdly funny even though you barely talk. And like I said, you just have this crazy soothing presence, which, okay, sounds way too fucking new-agey. Anyway, no. I'm not trying to like, get my rocks off with the hot farmer dude and then bail." Great. My voice was breaking, and I had officially fallen into a spiral of panicked rambling.

Matt's shoulders shook with silent laughter. "You're cute, Mikah." He brushed his lips over mine and everything uncoiled. His calming effect was immediate. He was so comfortable in his own body that he made me comfortable in mine by association. I almost wanted to lean back and say *see, you're doing it right now.* But then Matt's big hands cupped my neck, pulling me up to him, closer. The wind gusted around us, and I shivered with a mix of pleasure and cold. Matt's body was welcoming and solid, and all I wanted was to twine us so tightly together we could never be unwound.

"Will you stay?" I asked, breathing heavy against his mouth. His slow, easy smile warmed me through.

MY room, like the rest of the house, was chilly and quiet. It seemed everyone had drifted off to bed while Matt and I were out walking. Already I was fuzzy with arousal, clumsy as I pulled off my boots and too loud as I shut and locked my bedroom door.

"You're shivering." Matt rubbed my arms. "Want me to build a fire?"

Instinctively I wanted to argue that I could do it myself, but I paused. I liked that he wanted to do it. I liked his gentle concern and down-to-earth helpfulness. Matt lit the fire with quick, sure movements, the flames painting the room in a soft, flickering glow. In the firelight his hair was almost golden, the blue of his eyes deeper. Not wanting to stare at him, I glanced into the growing flames. Unbidden, I remembered burning Josh's letter, erasing the last vestige of my hurt in very spot where Matt was kneeling. A sharp realization pinged through me—as much as I'd been desperate to build something real with Josh, I'd never felt for him in three years what I felt for Matt after the one month we'd spent together.

"Come here," he requested, his words drawing me to him like his arms would. I eased myself down to sit across from him in front of the fire, knees touching as if we were kids ready to swap secrets. Then his arms did come around me, pulling me easily into his lap.

I wanted to know his body. So much of him was hard and rough, calloused hands and wind-burned cheeks, but I wanted to find the places where he was soft, to trace the thin, pale skin behind his ears with my tongue. I wanted to understand his steady, rhythmic calm, to take it into me. Sliding my hands under the fabric of his shirt, I touched the planes of his work-honed muscles. I liked Matt's body, its thickness and heft. And I wanted it all around me, pressing me down and filling me.

"That feels good," Matt breathed. He kissed me gently, brushing his lips over mine. A kiss so tender, I didn't know what to do with myself. I'd thought too much over the past month about sex with Matt, but now that fantasy was becoming reality, I was overwhelmed by my need for him. I buried my face into his neck, breathing his pine smell and the smoke of the fire, and the faintest hint of the cinnamon he'd stirred into his coffee. I must have mumbled something about him smelling good because he chuckled, the sound rumbling low in his chest.

"Had to cut a few trees this morning before we closed. The smell sticks to you. The sap."

"Mmm. I like it," I murmured and ran my tongue up the cord of his neck. Matt moaned. His hands went to my hips and squeezed.

"Mikah." Matt's voice was husky as I dotted kisses along the sharp line of his jaw. I liked the sound of my name in his mouth. "You're driving me crazy. I want you so much."

Angling my face to his, I connected our lips, opening him and sliding my tongue inside. Hot desire burned down my spine, leaving me panting and loose-limbed. I wanted Matt in my bed, but I didn't want our bodies to separate for even a fraction of a second. Happily, Matt solved this problem by scooping me up and rising to his feet in a motion so smooth I was forced to pull my mouth away to murmur my admiration. Wrapping my legs around him, I pushed my fingers into his close-cropped hair. The strands were thick and coarse. I didn't stop kissing him as he navigated the short distance to the bed. For a while—it could have been minutes or much longer—we kissed and ground together restlessly. His weight on top of me was everything I needed. I was throbbing for him, and I scrabbled at the button of my jeans. Matt eased off of me, eyes blazing and intent on my face.

"What do you like?" he asked, lifting my hand to press a kiss to the inside of my wrist. I wondered if he could feel my pulse racing there.

"You," I said without thinking, immediately embarrassed by my sappy admission. But Matt's blush and smile made me happy. My words, I realized, were a gift. They had the power to soothe such a steady, solid man.

"I like you too. A lot." He murmured the last two words so quietly I almost missed them. Matt kissed me hard and fast. "But do you, you know, normally top or bottom?"

"Both. I mean either way's good for me. Whatever." I didn't know where my sudden burst of discomfort was coming from. It certainly wasn't the first time I'd had this particular conversation.

Matt cupped my cheek and kissed me again so softly and sweetly, something deep inside me unraveled. "I'm flexible too. But I want to know what *you* want." He didn't seem at all uncomfortable, just waited patiently for my response.

"I want you to…." I stared down at the embroidery on the white duvet. I'd known what I wanted from the moment his thumb had brushed my lips in his cabin. "I want you to fuck me." As I spoke my desire aloud, heat curled in my belly, seeping into my thighs, leaving me achy with need. I wanted Matt everywhere.

"Okay," he said simply, sifting his fingers through my hair and pushing it back from my face.

I was grateful my fingers didn't tremble as I reached to undo the buttons on Matt's green flannel shirt. Underneath he wore a gray henley, and my mouth went dry at the sight of him tugging it over his head. He was powerfully muscled. His was the kind of body produced by manual labor. I loved the dusting of golden hair on his chest, so I kissed it, savoring the intimacy of warm skin under my lips. Dragging my mouth lower to Matt's tight stomach, I fumbled with the oversized buckle of his cowboyish leather belt. Of course he wore belts like this.

"Mikah…."

I shivered with delight when he said my name. "Uh-huh." I paused my motion and lifted my gaze to him but kept my face level with his crotch. I was breathing hard, desperate for him.

"I want to see you too." Matt tugged at the hem of my sweater.

Right. I was still fully dressed. I'd been so focused on getting Matt naked, I'd forgotten myself. With none of his suave, I yanked my sweater over my head and shimmied out of my jeans and underwear.

"You're so gorgeous," he said softly.

My heart leaped to my throat, and I resumed my mission to map every inch of his skin. When my fingers curled around his length, Matt made a needy whimper low in his throat. I bent to take him fully into my mouth, gripping his thick thighs to steady myself. Glancing up, I saw his eyes drift shut, head tipping up as I moved my mouth lower. The taste of him, salty and clean, sent hot sparks of pleasure over my skin.

"Oh, fuck. Baby, that's so good." Matt's voice was raw. My eyes burned at the term of endearment. Before I could keep going, though, he lay down on his back. I sat back on my heels for a minute, admiring his hard body and soft eyes. Then he pulled me down to lie on top of him and gripped my body hard with both hands. Our erections rubbed together, and I almost sobbed with the satiating thrill of contact.

"Please," I begged, unsure of what I was even asking for. Matt put two fingers to my lips, but it wasn't to quiet me. He slipped into my mouth, and I swirled my tongue to wet them. His cock twitched against mine, and he groaned. Then one finger was at my entrance, touching me gently.

"This okay?" Matt asked, his body completely still as he waited for my response.

"Yes. Please. Fuck." It was difficult to speak when my throat was burning with desire.

He sank into me, and we both moaned as I clenched around his finger. Shivery pleasure built within me as he slid a second finger inside. But I needed more. I was suddenly grateful that this morning I'd sheepishly tucked lube and some condoms into the drawer of my nightstand. I never wanted Matt to leave my bed.

"Matt, please. Now." I kissed him again for good measure and gestured to the small pine cabinet. Slowly he eased out of me and made quick work of locating the drugstore bag. I watched him, breath held, as he rolled the condom onto his thick length and slicked himself up with lube. Everything about him turned me on: the heat of his gaze, the sureness of his movements, the surprising tenderness of his kisses. My thighs tightened as he easily moved me so I was lying on my back, and draped his larger body over mine. I loved the simultaneous roughness and care of his touch.

Everything narrowed to the sensation of his mouth claiming me: ragged breaths, the taste of his skin, the thrill that shimmered down my body as his tongue slid against mine. Matt's strong fingers gripped my knees, pushing them back and opening me to him. I gasped at the hot spark of pleasure-pain as he eased into me, and whimpered at the fullness as Matt started to thrust. I felt so satisfied, I could barely think, much less breathe. As he moved faster, I was lost in the gratification of his heat inside me, brushing again and again over the spot that made me squeeze my eyes shut and bite my lip to keep from crying out. I reached for my own erection, but Matt linked his fingers with mine, pressing my hand down to the bed as he continued to drive into me. Skin slapped against skin, and he growled as I constricted around his length.

When he started stroking me, each movement somehow perfectly coordinated with his smooth thrusts, I realized I could no longer control my whimpers and pleas. I lifted my lips to his, and he grunted as our mouths connected.

"God, Mikah," Matt exhaled into my mouth. His grip tightened, and my hips surged up. A delicious, slick tension built deep inside, consuming me. All I could do was arch toward his touch, every cord of muscle in my body pulled tight. Then everything was liquid heat, detonating in my core and radiating through me. I was begging, delirious as I came. Spilling between us, grasping at Matt desperately, I tried to pull him as close as possible. Matt's arms snaked under me, pressing my chest flush against his. Surging once, hard, he came with a low, coarse moan.

I was wrung out and boneless, eyes still squeezed shut from my orgasm. When I squinted them open, Matt was there, staring down at me with such fondness that my eyes filled and my vision clouded. This intimacy overwhelmed me. Matt was rearranging the cells in my body. Every thin layers I'd wrapped around myself fell away in the soft warmth of his presence.

"Hey," Matt whispered, rubbing his thumb over my lips, "was that okay?"

I cleared my throat, knowing that my voice would be all weird and broken. "Um, yes. Why are you so good at sex?" I was glad I sounded teasing, instead of like I was going to dissolve into tears.

Matt treated me to his patented smirk before he slid out of me and wrapped the condom in a tissue. The fire was still roaring, but I shivered, immediately missing his heat. For a moment I lay still, enjoying the delicious soreness. I knew I needed to clean up and take care of practical things like getting Matt a toothbrush and pawing through my clothes to find anything that could possibly fit him, but all I wanted to do was lay my head on his chest and drift off to sleep. My practical side won out, and I darted to the en suite bathroom. When I emerged, Matt had pulled on his boxers and was leaning against the headboard, looking unfairly gorgeous but a little wary.

"Still okay if I spend the night?" he asked, not meeting my eyes.

I flopped into bed and straddled him, a huge grin on my face. "You better! I'm not done with your fine ass." I felt him relax beneath me. "Naomi puts, like, a million spare toothbrushes in every bathroom, so choose any color you'd like." I kissed the corner of his mouth.

As much as I wanted to be lighthearted and fun, the thought of Matt leaving in the morning made my chest feel hollow. I glanced at my dresser, mentally looking through the heavy pine drawers to where I'd stashed the tiny box wrapped in pretty gold paper. Maybe I should forget it. Giving Matt a Christmas gift was weird. Especially this one. Honestly, I didn't know what had come over me as I'd wrapped up the present. There was no denying that giving Matt this particular gift was… heavy. Just thinking of watching him open it made my stomach swoop, made me feel raw and vulnerable in exactly the way I worked hard to avoid. *This* was what my brother meant when he said I needed to be careful not to get too attached. And he was right. I wanted Matt too much. Because I didn't feel mistaken with him. It was easier to suppress the vulnerable parts of me, easier to coast through relationships with my defenses up so I didn't get hurt. The last time I let them down and opened myself up enough to feel, Josh had tossed me aside without a care. With Matt, though, I felt safe. I felt seen. I felt like I could learn his flaws and show him mine. I felt he was a man I could come to trust.

"Mikah?" Matt cupped my face with his callused hands. "Baby, what's wrong?"

I knew my emotional turmoil was probably plain in my expression, but I couldn't rustle up any shame. I stared at Matt's concerned, handsome face. In that moment, I surrendered, giving myself to him fully. But instead of crumbling, I opened. Between us there was nothing but truth.

"Sorry." I shook my head and focused my attention anywhere but Matt's face. "I, um, really like you a lot and... sorry...." I trailed off because my throat was getting all tight and hot.

"Hey." His voice was thick as he turned my face toward his. That shy smile was back, and it made me unbelievably happy to see. "You don't have to be embarrassed. I like you a lot too. Let's make the most of the time we have together, okay?" He made it sound so simple. I nodded, still feeling weepy as he kissed me hard and fast.

Matt disappeared to the bathroom to wash up and I lay in bed worrying I would keep him awake with my usual restless pillow punching and body flailing. Instead, when he came back to bed, he tugged me close against him, and I discovered that resting my head on his chest was even better than I'd imagined. Lulled into a state of deep relaxation by the gentle rise and fall of his breaths, I was hardly awake when I heard Matt's whispered words. "Merry Christmas, Mikah."

My response was lost, though, as I sank fully into the dark, placid waters of sleep.

Chapter Eight

Matt

OUTSIDE, snow drifted down against the windowpane. *A white Christmas.* I smiled to myself, thinking of how many times I'd listened to Elvis's version of the holiday classic. It played in my head, mingling with the soft sounds of Mikah's breath against my neck and the fizzy patter of snowflakes falling to the frozen ground outside. The air in the bedroom was just shy of uncomfortably cold, and I wondered if Mikah's dad relied fully on fireplaces to heat the cavernous house. The fire had died overnight, now nothing but a pile of ash in the stone hearth. Instead of getting up to rebuild it, though, I cuddled closer to Mikah.

He was, unsurprisingly, beautiful in his sleep, softer and almost innocent without his usual wry smirks and eyebrow raises. His hair covered half his face, and I couldn't deny myself the pleasure of trailing my fingers through it to reveal more of his creamy skin. I wanted to kiss his eyelashes and the tip of his nose, but I also wanted him to rest. This, I knew in my bones, was the happiest I'd been in a long time. It was probably the happiest I'd ever be. Again, the thought of building a future with Mikah filled me with a rising tide of warm joy. If I let the tide rise too high, I worried it might bubble up into a laugh that woke the man lying next to me. So instead I mentally listed the things Mikah and I could do together. Free of the obligation to cut down Christmas trees and tie pine boughs into attractive bundles, I could take Mikah skiing. We could go to my favorite restaurant in town. And I could finally cook for him, make him my famous meatloaf and garlic mashed potatoes. Okay, so not *famous*, but John and Katie and Abby liked it enough.

A slow, deep intake of breath next to me pulled me from my daydreams. Mikah's brown eyes blinked open, and he smiled softly when they met mine.

"Hey," he breathed, arching his back in an adorable morning stretch.

"Hi." I pressed my lips to his forehead. Mikah wrapped his arms around my neck, rolling to lie on top of me. I delighted in the brush of his slim thighs against mine, the weight of his chest on my own.

"Hmm, I like waking up with you." He smiled, half-playful, half-sincere.

"Me too." My hands drifted downward, and his eyes went wide.

"Do you want to?" Mikah writhed on top of me, and every part of my body woke right up.

As much as I wanted nothing more than to slip back inside him and stroke him until he was panting and crying out under me, the clatter of pans and smell the rich brown scent of coffee drifted up from the kitchen. Mikah seemed to take my silence as a rejection rather than a bookmark, though, and he slid off me, the mask of irony back on his face. It made me weirdly sad, the way he wore his indifference like armor. I would do anything I could to peel it away. Even the one thing I'd been so nervous about.

"I, uh, have something for you." Tugging on my discarded undershirt, I padded over to where I'd left my coat and the shopping bag the night before. I bit the inside of my cheek to hide a smile as I pulled out the large box, wrapped in brown paper and tied with the twine we used to bind the Christmas trees. Figuring it needed a little bit of color, I'd tucked a tiny spruce sprig into the bow. The tightness in Mikah's face dissolved. He looked so excited, I stopped worrying that he might not like the gift.

"Oh thank God!" His laugh was a bright, tinkling sound. "I have a present for you too. But I…. Anyway, that doesn't matter." He rummaged around in his dresser drawer before pulling out a small box. It was beautifully wrapped in gold paper with a holly motif and a glittery silver ribbon.

"Well, here ya go." I held out my gift to him, rubbing the back of my neck, which suddenly felt really hot.

Mikah reached out to accept it but at the last minute snapped his hand away like he'd been burned. Confused as hell, I dropped the present on the floor. Thankfully it wasn't breakable.

"Wait!" Mikah splayed his hands in front of him, shaking his head wildly. "We need to, like, set the scene." He nodded, mind made up, looking way too cute in only his plaid pajama bottoms.

"What do you have in mind?" I asked, laughing and gesturing to the window. "It's already snowing."

"Okay. Maybe you can build a fire, because it's fucking freezing in this house all the time. And *I* will go get us some coffee. Oh! And panettone! Yes!" His excitement was contagious.

Warmth built in my chest that had nothing to do with the fire as I held a match to a careful arrangement of newspaper and birch logs. If only every Christmas could be like this, every morning for that matter: waking up with Mikah wrapped around me, his citrusy smell and softly parted lips greeting me as I came into the world.

"Sorry that took so long." Mikah hipped the door closed behind him. I hurried to take both coffee mugs from his hands. A plate balanced precariously on his forearm, and I was impressed that he hadn't dropped anything. "My dad wanted us to come have coffee with him in the kitchen. But no one else is even up yet. Well, Luca probably is, but I bet he's working." He rolled his eyes.

I took a sip of my coffee, and a new tendril of affection for Mikah unfurled in me. He'd made it exactly right, with cinnamon and sugar. I watched as he arranged pillows in front of the fire, placing both gifts and the plate loaded with some kind of bread or cake between them. With a flourish he gestured for me to sit down. I sat and took a grateful bite of the cake. I'd eaten so much the night before, I'd wondered if I would even be able to enjoy any of the elaborate Christmas

Day brunch Katie made every year. But I was starving. And this was delicious, soft and buttery with raisins and what tasted like orange.

"You like the panettone?" Mikah's gaze was intent on my face. I nodded, mouth too full to answer. His cheeks went pink. "This is the first time I made it. My nonna usually does that too. Are you sure you like it?"

I leaned forward to kiss him, tasting coffee and a hint of toothpaste on his lips. "I'm sure. It's really good."

"Mmmm. Tastes good on you." Mikah waggled his eyebrows, and I shook my head.

"Here. Will you open this now?" I handed him the present again, this time holding it with two hands.

Mikah accepted it with a goofy grin, shaking the box and peering at it. His eyes went liquid, and he reached to squeeze my knee. "Matt, you really didn't have to get me a gift. Thank you."

"Don't thank me yet," I grumbled. "You don't even know what it is."

Beaming, he methodically untied the twine and peeled away the tape. Wondering if the extra care was for my benefit made my stomach drop—I loved seeing this sweet, attentive side to Mikah. Once he'd taken his time folding the wrapping paper into a perfect square and set it aside, he squealed in delight and hugged the black Carhartt coat, a Mikah-sized version of my own brown one, to his chest.

"So you don't freeze to death. And this one will actually fit you," I explained, looking intently at the fire.

But I could see him out of the corner of my eye, unfolding the thick black material and draping the coat over his shoulders. "Thank you so much! I love it! And—" He broke off, suddenly looking embarrassed. "This is awesome."

"I'm glad you like it." The fire popped, a shower of sparks rising up with the smoke. I glanced down at the small present between us. "Can I open it, or…?"

Mikah rolled his eyes and shoved it toward me. "Ugh. Yes. Here, just… it's superweird, so don't get your hopes up."

Gently I slid the ribbon off the box. My fingers shook a little as I peeled away the paper. I didn't get many gifts. John and Katie usually gave me clothes or CDs even though I told them every year not to worry about getting me a present. I always looked forward to Abby's gifts, though, which included homemade ornaments, painted rocks, and, last year a watercolor portrait of Moose now proudly displayed in my living room.

I'd had some nice surprises in my life: making the varsity football lineup my freshman year, Dylan Lloyd kissing me when I dropped him off after the state fair, my brother being so supportive of me being gay. But nothing had ever surprised me like Mikah's gift. Resting on a puffy square of cotton was his grandfather's necklace. The night before, I'd been so preoccupied with pleasure, I hadn't even noticed Mikah wasn't wearing it. But glancing at his chest, bare under the coat, I saw that the gold chain was no longer around his neck. I cleared my throat hard, the telltale prickle in my sinuses warning that I was about to cry.

"If you don't want to wear it, seriously no worries. I mean, you bought me a *coat,* and I just gave you something I already owned…." He sounded nervous, his voice tight and thin.

Mikah's words died as I hauled him into my lap and crushed my mouth to his. He made a startled sound in his throat before relaxing against me, the coat sliding off his shoulders. When our lips parted, both of us were breathing fast and heavy.

"This is the nicest present I've ever gotten," I said, meaning it. I lifted the necklace out of the box. The firelight danced on the polished gold, making it look molten. "Will you put it on me?" My voice was gravel-rough.

Mikah nodded seriously and, without climbing off my lap, reached around my neck to hook the clasp. As soon as it was around my neck, I knew I would never take it off. He patted the pendant and smiled.

"I know that this"—he gestured between the two of us—"might just be for now. But I want you to remember it. Remember me…." He cleared his throat. "Anyway, sorry if it's a weird gift. Seriously, don't feel obligated to wear it if you don't want to." His voice dropped so low it was barely a whisper.

When things got emotional, it got hard for me to talk. I preferred to communicate with my actions instead of words. But right now I knew Mikah needed both. Gripping his shoulders tight, I tipped my head down to connect our gazes.

"Of course I'll wear it. Mikah, you mean so much to me…." Speaking got difficult then, so I brushed my lips over his. What started as a gentle kiss grew hungry. I was light-headed with affection, with wanting him, but I knew I had to head home. When I pulled away, Mikah's needy whimper almost destroyed my last shred of resolve to go to my brother's brunch.

"Are you sure you have to go?" Mikah intuited.

Nodding, I kissed him one more time for good measure. "What are your plans today?" I pulled Mikah to his feet as I stood. Immediately he stepped between my legs and kissed the necklace where it lay against my chest. My heartbeat faltered.

"I think Naomi's making 'healthy' pancakes." Mikah made a dubious face. "So you're probably wise not to stick around for those. After that, not much. Christmas Eve is the bigger deal for us. We'll open presents later, maybe watch movies and eat leftovers." He shrugged lightly. "You?"

"My brother's hosting a brunch. It'll be a bunch of John's hunting buddies and Katie's teacher friends. My sister-in-law makes a mean french toast casserole, though, so it's worth the small talk. And I want to give my niece her present." I couldn't wait to see Abby's face when she opened the geology kit I'd special-ordered months ago.

Mikah nodded, and I could tell he was about to slip back into his indifferent mask.

"If you're not doing anything tonight, you want to come over for dinner? I can cook for you. Nothing as nice as you put together last night, but—"

"Yes! Please." Mikah threw his arms around me.

I CLIMBED into my truck, now coated in a few more inches of powdery snow. I buzzed with energy, my leg bouncing, teeth chattering from the frigid air. My lips kept twitching into a smile, and I didn't want it to go away. George Strait started crooning "Silent Night" the moment I turned the key in the ignition. I sang along at top volume, not even caring when a group of women in a fancy SUV giggled at me as I glided to a halt next to them at a stoplight. I was happy. Giving them a quick wave, I mouthed, "Merry Christmas," before turning off toward the Teton Pass. As I approached the road that would take me from Wyoming to Idaho, cars turned around, meaning the pass was closed because of the heavy snow. Usually, this discovery would have me muttering curses under my breath and tensing my jaw. Today, though, I shrugged it off, cranked up my music, and turned to take the long way home.

Pulling up outside the modest two-bedroom ranch where John and I grew up, I realized the jigsaw of minivans and trucks in the gravel driveway meant I would have to park a good hundred yards from the house. How the hell did John and Katie have so many friends? If I'd been thinking, I would have parked at home. But I was excited to give Abby her present. And I was starving. As I trudged through the snow to the front door, which was outlined in blinking colored lights and adorned with a huge fir wreath, Moose barked from inside. Abby pulled the door open, wearing some kind of superhero costume and waving wildly.

"Merry Christmas, Uncle Matt!"

I scooped her into my arms, lifting her high overhead. "Merry Christmas, bug." I set her down inside the threshold and shrugged out of my jacket. "How was your grandma's?"

Abby twisted her shoulders and scrunched her nose. She looked like a miniature version of her mother, with shiny black hair and tawny skin. "It was okay. Auntie Mary wears too much perfume." Moose padded up behind her, and I bent to scratch his head.

I laughed, grateful I'd taken a shower before leaving Mikah's so I wouldn't be subject to the same scrutiny.

"Merry Christmas, bro!" John strolled into the small entryway, wearing a truly hideous green-and-red sweater. His dark hair was dusted with snow.

"Oh dang, was this an ugly sweater party?" I teased.

"Grandma made it for him," Abby informed me. John nodded grimly. Every year Katie's mom knitted them holiday sweaters, and somehow John's was always the ugliest.

I followed them into the living area. It was hard to believe this was the same house I'd been raised in. John had cleaned the place up after our parents passed, scrubbing the yellowed linoleum in the kitchen and ridding the house of the piles of old magazines and unread junk mail. But when Katie moved in, she whipped the place into shape. The dingy flooring was replaced with wide-plank reclaimed wood, and the once off-white walls were now painted a variety of bright colors. The house smelled different too. Gone was the tang of stale beer and neglected dishes. Katie always burned cinnamon candles, making the place feel warm and cozy. The kitchen was full of Katie's friends, chatting and helping my sister-in-law put the finishing touches on brunch.

"Hey, stranger!" Katie shook off her oven mitts and wrapped me in a big hug. She looked pretty, in fitted jeans and a much more toned-down sweater with a snowflake pattern. "You have a good time at your boyfriend's place?"

Not wanting to sound fifteen in front of a bunch of strange women, I bit back the *he's not my boyfriend* retort and nodded.

"You got a boyfriend?" Abby asked excitedly. "Did he give you that necklace?"

My hand flew automatically to my chest, and I could feel myself blushing as I tucked it under my shirt. "Yup."

"Oh, really?" Katie eyed me shrewdly.

Desperate to evade the coming inquisition, I grabbed a muffin from a tray on the concrete breakfast bar dividing the kitchen from the den. It was gross, though: store-bought and sickly sweet. I turned my

attention back to my niece. "So what did Santa bring?"
I asked. I'd given the wrapped geology kit to Katie the
morning before, and she'd promised me Abby wouldn't
open it until I came over.

Abby ticked the gifts off on her fingers. "Umm,
some books, and an art set, and a new nightlight, and,
uhh… oh! A dog lovie that looks like Moose!" She
pointed to a stuffed Bernese Mountain Dog tossed
haphazardly on the plaid sofa.

"It does look like Moose," I agreed. "You gonna
name it Moose Jr.?"

Abby furrowed her brows at the suggestion. "No.
His name is Gunther." She sighed like this should have
been obvious. Katie nodded seriously.

"Well, I got you something too." I cut my eyes
over to the Christmas tree in the corner of the den,
circled with a popcorn garland and exploding with
tinsel. Clearly, Abby had a large hand in decorating it.

"The big one?" Abby darted to grab the gift, tearing
excitedly at the paper before I could even respond. "What?"
she shrieked as she unzipped the canvas backpack storing
the rock-collecting kit and pulled out the various tools and
magnifying glasses. "Thankyouthankyouthankyou!"

"This is a real geology kit. So you need to be
careful with the tools, okay?" I gave Abby the sternest
look I could muster in the face of her delight. She had
slipped on the safety goggles, which were a little too
big for her face.

"Do you want to give Uncle Matt his present?"
Katie said to her daughter pointedly. With obvious
reluctance Abby tucked the kit back into the backpack
and rummaged through the remaining pile of gifts for
mine, clumsily wrapped in cartoon reindeer paper.

"I wonder what it could be." I grinned at my niece.

"You know." Abby shook her head, exasperated.

This year's ornament was made of bright green beads and pipe cleaners. It was some kind of animal, long, skinny, and four legged. Giving it an appreciative nod, I tucked it carefully back into the recycled cookie box it came in.

"Thanks, bug." I bent to kiss the top of her head. "It's a real nice... crocodile?" I knew I was probably getting it wrong.

Abby scoffed. "It's a *dog*."

Usually when I came to gatherings at my brother's house, everyone seemed to segregate along gender lines. Most of the women hung out in the kitchen, chatting amiably and putting together trays of pastries or appetizers. The men congregated in the barn if it was nice out, or if it was cold, like today, in the heated garage. I never really felt comfortable anywhere and tended to walk back and forth between the two rooms so much, I worked up a sweat. When I drifted into the garage, it was crowded with John's friends, most of them drinking coffee but a few already nursing beers. John, who never drank, was sitting in a camping chair and watching a football game on the portable TV resting on his workbench.

"Hey, Matt." I turned to find Dylan Lloyd, my first crush, first kiss, first everything, leaning against the chest freezer. Dylan, whose deeply conservative family ran a sporting goods store a few towns over, was profoundly, heartbreakingly closeted. He was taller than me, which honestly was rare, and handsome with close-cropped dark hair and a charming smile. Because no one but me and his younger sister knew he was gay, he was the object of a lot of misdirected flirting and speculation around town. We got together from time to time, but even though he was a nice guy, I hated the secrecy of it. I wanted a partner, not a hookup who refused to look me in the eye after we both got off.

Being with him just wasn't enough. I wanted exactly what I'd found with Mikah.

"Hey," I said belatedly. I wanted to brush my fingers against Mikah's necklace, but I stuffed my hands into my pockets instead.

"Good Christmas?" Dylan took a long sip of beer.

I shrugged. "Not bad. You?" He grunted in response. Neither of us were stellar conversationalists.

Glancing around, he dropped his voice low. "Have any plans for tonight?"

My heart broke for him and, a little bit, for myself. "Yup."

"Oh, is Mikah comin' over?" John piped up from behind me. Had he been listening to my nonconversation with his friend? Surprise registered on Dylan's face. I said nothing.

"My little bro got himself a real cute boyfriend." John beamed. Everyone knew I was gay, but not everyone was comfortable with it. John, though, had zero tolerance for snide remarks or hatred in his house. "The dude came to buy a tree from us, and next thing I know, Matt was skipping out on work, and they were gettin' hot and heavy."

I shot my asshole brother a glare but refused to show any other signs of discomfort. A few guys mumbled what sounded like *cool*, and everyone else returned their attention pointedly to the game.

Dylan was staring at his hiking books, his grip on his beer bottle tight. When his hazel eyes met mine, I tried to communicate my apology without words. Unable to stop myself, my fingers closed around the necklace, and I let myself feel it all: the yearning, the affection, the desperate hope that Mikah could stay with me.

Chapter Nine

Matt

NOTHING had changed in my cabin since I locked the door behind me the day before, but emptiness echoed through the space as I flicked on the lights. My work boots were still on the doormat where I left them. The maple countertops were scrubbed clean, bare of clutter aside from the single unwashed coffee mug next to the sink. The woven blue-and-white rug Moose always slept on still needed to be vacuumed. Since I'd been away overnight, the familiar smell of my house was more noticeable, the lingering scent of fresh-cut lumber and woodsmoke almost overwhelming. Although the place was small, just a combination living room–kitchen, my bedroom, the bathroom, and the spare room I used as an office and weight room, now the high ceilings and exposed timber beams yawned hollow and stark.

Crossing the room in wool-socked feet to add my new ornament to the Christmas tree, I reminded myself that Mikah would be here tonight, in my bed and in my arms. My nervous, excited energy was back in full force, so I hurried to tidy up, throwing away old leftovers, changing my sheets, mopping the floors with pine soap. By the time I'd finished scrubbing every last floorboard and dusting every available surface, I still had two hours before Mikah would be coming over for Christmas dinner.

I needed music. Moose eyed me from his post in front of the woodstove as I huffily riffled through CDs. Nothing in my exhaustive library of classic country matched the energy burning through my body. For the first time in a while, I wished I'd replaced my laptop when it died a few months earlier. I wanted to listen to Mikah's music, classical piano. Dragging my hand through my hair, I wracked my brain for the name of the song he'd played last night. Something with flowers? Flower dance? Finally, irritated with myself, I turned off my stereo and listened to nothing but the crackle of the fire and the whispering of the wind through the trees.

By the time the gravel in my driveway crunched beneath the wheels of Mikah's car, my cabin was the cleanest it had ever been. Moose and I watched through the wide windows as Mikah kicked the driver's side door shut behind him and yanked up the zipper on his new coat. At the sight of Mikah's narrow frame trudging through the drifts of snow, Moose's tail started wagging in wild circles, and he gave a tiny bark. I closed my eyes for a moment because it was all too much. Tenderness for Mikah swept through me, and when I pulled the door open, all I wanted was to wrap him up in my arms and hold him close. Instead, I stepped aside and offered him a small smile.

A blast of cold air and a flurry of snow followed Mikah into the cabin. His hair was even messier than usual, like he'd been running his fingers through it the whole drive over. He had a red nylon backpack slung over one shoulder, which I hoped meant he planned to spend the night.

"Coat warm enough?" I asked, sliding the snow-dusted Carhartt jacket off his fine-boned shoulders and hanging it on a hook next to the door. Mikah was adorably disheveled, jeans sprung at the knees, sweater stretched out and torn at the neck, black boots sloppily laced. It seemed like he'd gotten dressed in a rush. I wondered if his clothes came this way, predestroyed, or maybe he was just really bad at taking care of his stuff.

Mikah pressed up on the balls of his feet to kiss me. "It's perfect," he said against my lips. There was need in this kiss, but not the desperation to get off that colored so many of my sporadic hookups. It felt like he needed *me*. I wrapped my arms around him and squeezed him tight, my skin singing with satisfaction.

"Is it weird that I missed you?" Mikah asked, glancing up at me.

"Nope." I cupped his face, tilting his mouth toward mine again. He whined as our lips met. I couldn't get enough of his kisses, the smoothness of his lips, the way he grabbed at my shirt to pull me closer. I trailed a hand down the rough fabric of his sweater to his flat stomach. Dropping my fingers lower to the waistband of his pants, I slowly traced along the black denim, then the elastic band of his briefs. With a soft gasp, he pressed up on me, trying to force my hand in deeper. My fingertips grazed the warm, firm head of his erection.

"Matt." Mikah breathed my name. I wanted to hear him say it again.

"Hmm?" I dragged my mouth from his to kiss his cheeks, his eyebrows, his jaw.

"Can we get in bed?"

I shivered and nodded, already throbbing with anticipation and the memories of the night before, as we walked the short distance to my bedroom. We undressed quickly. Heat washed over me at the way Mikah watched as I shed my jeans and henley and underwear. His eyes were hungry, sleepy, and heavy-lidded. They went wide as they landed on the necklace, and he stepped close to draw me into a soft kiss. His lips drifted down my neck to my chest, kissing the skin right next to the pendant. Desire twisted through me when the flat of his tongue dragged over my nipple.

After pushing him gently onto the bed, I lay on top of him, letting the full weight of my body press him into the flannel sheets. Mikah cried out and held on to my shoulders hard. He liked that. I had never been with a man like Mikah, so giving and present in bed. I loved how responsive he was, his pleasure heightening my own in a delirious feedback loop.

Mikah squirmed under my body, kissing me feverishly and sighing softly as I shifted so our erections slid together. "What do you want?" He was looking intently at my face, eyes wide, like he wanted to give me everything.

My throat clicked as I swallowed. How many times had I thought about being asked this very question, absolutely sure fantasy would never become reality? I let my hands drift down to the curve of his ass.

"You want to fuck me?" Mikah nodded slowly, eyes fluttering closed.

"Yeah. But first I want…." I didn't know how to put it, so I squeezed the small, firm mound of muscle, delighting in the creamy tight expanse of his skin. I was so turned-on already, I felt like I could come apart.

"Oh." Mikah's eyes snapped open and his breath hitched. "Do you mean rimming?"

The last thing I wanted was to pressure him into anything he wasn't into, plus I didn't exactly know what I was doing, so I started to backtrack. "If you don't want to—"

Mikah crushed his mouth to mine. "Yes. I *very* much want that."

Easing back onto my knees, I turned him over and admired his smooth, slim body. Just looking at him made me light-headed and needy. Knowing he wanted me as much as I wanted him was almost overwhelming. Starting at a small constellation of freckles near the base of his neck, I kissed and licked my way down Mikah's spine. I wanted to feel and taste every inch of his skin, wanted to tend to him the way I would a plot of newly turned earth. Mikah whined and arched into me as I licked at his ass. His quiet gasps and citrus soap smell stoked my lust, my whole body alive with desire. This was better than I'd ever imagined. Part of me wanted to keep going until he was pliant and begging, but I also ached to be inside him. When I slid a spit-slicked finger into him, Mikah tensed and worry flooded me.

"You okay?" My voice was ragged.

"Yes," Mikah panted, clenching around me. "I... I, uh, need a second. Fuck, this is embarrassing. I don't usually get this worked up."

I kept still, not wanting to hurt him, and gently stroked my other hand up the notches of his spine. As much as I wanted to, I couldn't hold back my question. "Was that... not good? Obviously I've never done it before, so...." I trailed off, exposed and a little raw, but not ashamed. Mostly I wished I didn't have to ask.

"Matt." Mikah turned so his face was pressed into a pillow. His words came out muffled. "I was, like, two seconds from coming. It felt amazing. I really want you to fuck me."

Without thinking, I moved my finger inside him, curling it slightly. Mikah gasped.

"Now, please." His voice was thready.

Seeing him so acquiescent and wanting pressed a hot brand of lust to my skin. Something in me snapped, and my mind was sharp and clear, totally present.

"Get up on your hands and knees for me, baby," I suggested, and Mikah complied immediately. Even though I was almost painfully aroused, I took a moment to watch him, the way the late-afternoon sun filtering through the curtains rendered his mess of dark curls even shinier and softer than usual, the way his eyes locked with mine when he turned to look at me. We both grinned. Quickly, I rolled on a condom and slicked myself with lube. "You ready?" I asked, pressing a fast kiss to the back of his neck.

"Please, Matt—" Mikah's body shook like a leaf when I touched him. "Yes."

I slicked myself and slipped into him slowly, gripping his narrow waist hard. Breathing slow and steady, I watched the sharp bones of his shoulder blades relax before pushing in deeper. He shifted his hips and sighed my name, his body and words asking for more. My world was a hot swath of white. He was incredibly tight, slick velvet clenching around me as I pumped steadily in and out of him. I was losing control. Heat unfurled low in my belly. Twitching muscles in my thighs pointed toward orgasm. But something basic in me needed to see Mikah's release, to hear his broken cries, to watch as he came apart. I could feel him getting close.

"Touch yourself," I told him, and again Mikah obeyed without hesitation. My erection seemed to thicken inside him as shivery pleasure pooled at the base of my spine. He was trembling now, murmuring an incoherent stream of profanities. I moved faster, drove into him harder. Then Mikah's breathy moans and rocking back on me stopped. He clenched tight around my length, coming with a sharp cry before the arm holding him up gave out, and he collapsed down onto the bed. Needing him as close as possible, I hauled Mikah back up, bending over him to kiss the nape of his neck. His hair was damp, his skin salty with sweat. As I sank in deeper, his hot grip surrounded me, tipping me into oblivion. Two more hard thrusts, and it was over. My orgasm tore through me, leaving only tingling relief in its wake.

As I eased out of Mikah, he winced slightly, quickly cleaning up, then flopping back into the pile of pillows with a contented sigh. He threw his arms over his eyes and groaned. I was laughing, peppering kisses on Mikah's face and chest and neck. Sex had never been like that before, had never made me feel so right and whole.

Mikah's delicate fingers closed around my wrist, tugging me close next to him, wrapping us both in the warm nest of sheets. As soon as I lay down, he burrowed into my embrace. I smiled. Looking at Mikah outside the bedroom, with his arms perpetually crossed over his chest and ever-present cynical smiles on his refined face, I never would have imagined he was so snuggly. But, clearly, the guy loved to cuddle. He ran his fingers over me, slow and gentle, tracing tiny patterns on my skin.

A soft silence drifted down between us. The sheer-white curtains were closed, but through the small gap between them, I made out the golden glow of a setting sun. I always looked forward to watching the sunset. It seemed like the weather had cleared and part of me wanted to slide out of bed to open the curtains fully so I could watch as the sky faded to purple. But Mikah's legs tangled with mine, and the gentle kisses he pressed to my shoulder made my bed too perfect to leave.

"What are you doing to me?" Mikah murmured, his voice a little sleepy.

"I could ask you the same." I chuckled, turning to him so I could kiss the top of his head. Suddenly, though, my heart hammered in my chest, and I was struck by how much I liked being with Mikah, by the perfection of this moment. It wasn't just the sex. It wasn't just the fact that Mikah seemed to have an endless knowledge of musicians, writers, and artists I'd never heard of. It wasn't the way catching the faintest hint of Mikah's smell made my stomach light and heart race. It was the fact that we cared for each other. I could feel it in every brush of his skin against mine, hear it every time he said my name. I was in bed with a beautiful man who wanted *me*. A man I wanted so deeply, it was hard to wrap my head around. I was amazed that Mikah and I had found each other, that in the wide universe of possibility, someone so gorgeous and interesting and plain wonderful existed.

Mikah kissed me again, hard and firm like he'd come to some kind of private decision, but I wasn't quite sure what that might be. Heat bloomed on my neck, and I rubbed at it automatically. For another long moment, we lay in the quiet, watching the light shift and wane as the sun dipped below the mountains outside. I was starting to think Mikah may have drifted off to sleep when he turned to me, grinning, and asked, "So what are you making me for dinner?"

Chapter Ten

Mikah

"UM, what is this thing?" I gestured to the beaded ornament hanging front and center on Matt's small Christmas tree. It looked like some kind of fucked-up, surrealist green dog. While the rest of Matt's house was tidy and cozy—whitewashed wood walls, comfortable but simple furniture, minimal clutter—his Christmas tree looked like a grade-school art room exploded all over it. Every ornament was handmade and brightly colored. A few included choppily cut photos of Matt and a tiny dark-haired girl who I assumed was his niece.

"Apparently it's a dog. My guess that it was a crocodile did *not* go over too well with Abby." Matt mock-grimaced from his post behind the counter. But his face went soft at the mention of his niece. He was too charming for his own good.

I quickly snapped my attention back to the tree. In addition to being an adorably devoted uncle, he'd pushed up the sleeves of his dark green henley, revealing thickly muscled forearms that flexed with his every movement. Probably it would read as slightly creepy for me to stare at him slack-jawed as he made dinner. Really, watching him, calm and precise, as he chopped vegetables and reached for pans was incredibly distracting. So distracting in fact, that I'd almost cut my thumb off trying to mince some garlic and had been banished to relaxing in front of the blazing woodstove with Moose.

Although I'd only been in Matt's cabin a handful of times, the place was so cozy that it already felt homier than the majority of the places I'd lived in the past. The SoHo apartment I grew up in was always pristine, with fresh-from-the-showroom designer furniture arranged just so and big abstract prints adorning every wall. I'd only felt at ease in the poster-collaged confines of my bedroom. My college dorm and subsequent shared apartment had been pleasantly chaotic, but both were transient spaces filled with mismatched, disposable furniture. Really, my one-bedroom walkup in Cambridge with its view of traffic-clogged Mass Ave and clanking radiators had been the closest I'd ever gotten to my idea of home. I'd been sad to leave as I loaded my clothes and books into my car for the multiday road trip out to Jackson the month before. Now that I was gone, though, I didn't miss the place.

Here, though, my shoulders relaxed as the smell of fresh pine mingled with the delicious aroma of the onions and herbs Matt was sautéing in butter. I snuggled into the shirt I'd borrowed for a second time, surreptitiously sniffing the soft cotton that smelled like Matt. After getting distracted from the what's-for-dinner conversation by a make-out session that turned into a second round of sex, I'd been so sleepy and content that the idea of changing back into my stiff jeans and scratchy sweater seemed nearly impossible. So I'd asked Matt if he had something comfy I could put on. I kind of had a thing for wearing his clothes. Now, my body had the soft floaty sensation of a fever breaking. Everything was bright and hazy and perfect, like being pleasantly tipsy, although I'd had nothing to drink. I smiled to myself when I realized this was what people must mean when they said they felt *totally relaxed*. I'd never really felt that way before. Scratching Moose's head, I leaned back against the couch and allowed my eyes to drift out of focus as I stared at the Christmas tree. The white lights expanded over the spots of color and dark boughs of green, everything merging into a glimmering blur.

"You sure your family's okay with you being over here on Christmas?" Matt's voice pulled my attention back to the kitchen. He'd moved on to peeling potatoes, and I stood, hoping he would actually let me help. When I gestured for him to give me the paring knife, he shrugged and handed it over carefully, handle first.

"Oh, for sure." I laughed. My dad and Naomi were going to a vegan dinner party at the ultramodern home of the woman who co-owned the yoga studio with my stepmom. Elena, in a rare moment of anxiousness, hadn't even looked up from her laptop as I walked out the door to leave for Matt's place. She'd been mumbling all afternoon about needing to get work done on some big collaborative structural dynamics project. Luca, as usual, was determined to catch up on emails.

"Seriously, Christmas Eve is the big holiday for us. So no worries at all. If I were at home I'd probably just be, like, marathoning the Harry Potter movies and taking BuzzFeed quizzes."

"This is a nice change of pace," Matt admitted, his eyes locked on the winter greens he'd started meticulously chopping into thin, even strips. "Christmas is usually pretty quiet for me. Kinda nice not to be by myself."

Something went hollow in my chest at his words. Gently, I set down the potato I was peeling and wrapped my arms around Matt, pressing my chest into his back as close as possible. If I could, I would leach away whatever made his voice go low and distant.

"This is nice for me too," I said into the broad expanse of his back. "I like hanging out with you a lot." This was a massive understatement. With the exception of my family, spending time with others tended to drain me. Sometimes I'd enjoyed grabbing a quick cocktail with a friend or going for a jog with a fellow teacher after school, but more than a few hours of prolonged human contact rendered me desperate for the quiet of a cozy chair and a novel. With Matt, though, the time flowed by, easy and gentle. I actively craved his presence. I could imagine myself sprawled on the couch, with my feet in his lap, both of us reading or talking for hours. But my heart stammered at the realization that this cozy tableau was only temporary. I was leaving. In a little over a week I would be back in New York, camping out at my mom's place and making pleasant conversation with her steady stream of aggressively chic friends.

Still plastered to Matt's back, I burrowed my face into his warmth and matched my breathing to his. Long inhale, slow exhale. After a moment he turned to face me, his gaze tender. So tender, in fact, that my heart started to pound in my chest, and I lost the even pace of my breaths. But then his lips quirked up, and he bent down, pressing his lips to mine.

"You like chocolate chip cookies?" he asked when we parted.

"Yeah. My mom used to get these amazing ones from this French bakery on the Upper West Side. She still sends me boxes of them a few times a year."

"Okay, well, I don't think these will be *that* fancy. But chocolate chip cookies are kinda my specialty. Want to help?" Matt chuckled, nodding in the direction of flour, eggs, and butter laid out on the counter.

"Cool!" I grinned, genuinely excited. "I've never made chocolate chip cookies before."

Matt shot me a skeptical look. "I thought you liked baking?"

"I do. Just, I make Italian stuff for the most part. And chocolate chip cookies aren't exactly a Sicilian staple."

"Well, these are pretty much the only thing I know how to bake. People seem to like 'em fine. We even bring them to the market sometimes." Matt actually looked a little sheepish, color rising to his cheeks. He really was too adorable. I wanted to kiss him, so I did, pressing up onto my tiptoes to ghost my lips over his. In addition to being unreasonably handsome, Matt was ridiculously tall, so it was hard to reach his mouth without him bending his knees.

"Why are you so tall?" I grumbled, reaching for the red-and-white mixing bowl next to the cookie supplies.

Matt ignored my question, instead handing me the bag of flour and instructing me to measure out two and a half cups while he checked on the meatloaf in the oven. I felt happy, almost silly, in a way I hadn't since I was a little kid. As Matt turned to provide me with further cookie instructions, I blew a tiny cloud of flour at his face. For a moment he looked shocked. His blond eyebrows, lightly dusted with white, shot toward his adorably rumpled hair. Then he grabbed me by the waist and lifted me onto the counter. I lost myself in the sensation of his lips on mine. It was a good thing he'd set a timer on the oven.

MATT fussed with his stereo for a long time, clearly deliberating over the music, before we settled onto stools at the counter to eat. I'd never really liked country music or meatloaf very much before, but in Matt's warm, cozy cabin, both were perfect. Plus the meatloaf was actually delicious. The food, like the man who made it, was wholesome and hearty. Matt grew the potatoes and winter greens himself, and his brother, apparently, had hunted the elk for the meatloaf. I joked that a farm-to-table meal like this would probably cost about fifty dollars a plate in New York, and Matt looked appalled. We chatted nonstop as we ate, about how he'd adopted Moose after some skiers abandoned the dog in town two winters ago, about how he and John built his timber frame cabin themselves, about the trials and tribulations of my solo road trip from Cambridge to Jackson in November. The conversation lulled to a comfortable silence, and Matt finished the food on my plate. He'd served me far more than I could possibly eat in a single sitting. I leaned forward against the countertop, relaxed and satisfied, running my fingers over the fine, light wood grain and tapping my foot along with the music.

"Huh," I said suddenly. Matt glanced up from polishing off the rest of my potatoes. "I never would have thought I'd enjoy country Christmas music of all things. Who is this?"

A flash of enthusiasm transformed Matt's stoic face. "Loretta Lynn. She's great, isn't she? My mom was a huge fan. Had a picture of her tucked into the frame of her mirror and everything."

My head buzzed with questions about Matt's family, but I had an inkling that he didn't really like being asked about his upbringing. So I just nodded enthusiastically and kept quiet. After a long moment, he continued, his words steady and measured.

"My mom was a good lady. She had a hard time. Both my parents did. They were always big drinkers, regulars at all the local dives. But when I was in middle school, it got worse. My dad got hurt shoeing one of the horses. Fell and messed up his back. The pills the doctor gave him, well, I guess he and my mom liked them a little too much. They started drinking more too… and things changed. Farm started suffering." Matt turned toward me, unwilling to meet my eye. I had no idea what to say, but I was glad Matt felt comfortable opening up to me. I listened, scooting my stool a little closer to him but giving him space in case he wanted it. But he closed the gap between us, hauling me into a tight embrace. This time when he took me into his arms, it felt different. Like I could give him back some of the calm he'd poured into me.

"You don't have to talk about this if you don't want to." I spoke carefully. As much as I wanted to give Matt room to share, I also didn't want to pry.

"Shit, I want to tell you. It's… embarrassing, I guess. My family wasn't like yours. We didn't talk and cook together. Hell, John and I pretty much raised ourselves." Matt released me and folded his arms over his broad chest.

Standing, I gripped Matt's shoulders and relaxed my features, hoping to show him with my body that he could say anything to me. I bent to look in his eyes, shifting so he couldn't avoid my gaze. "Matt," I said as softly as possible, "I want to know everything about you. You don't have to act a certain way around me. And please don't be embarrassed. Just because your parents struggled with addictions does *not* mean they were bad people. That doesn't make you a bad person."

Matt hesitated. "Look, I'm not trying to make a big deal of this. The past is the past. But I mean, when they died they didn't leave anything good behind." His fingers flew to the necklace, brushing over it gently. He was still breathing steadily, calmly, but his gaze remained fixed on the floor. "The farm, the house, and some debt. That's it." Moose, who had been snoozing next to Matt's feet, leapt to follow as he stalked into the kitchen with our plates.

"Matt...." I started, close behind, wanting to hold him.

"Mikah, you went to Harvard. I didn't even finish high school. I'm lucky I love farming because I can't do anything else."

"That doesn't matter, though," I said, rushing to set him at ease. Now Matt was visibly upset, jaw twitching with tension that I felt in my own body. "Like who gives a shit where I went to college?" I bit my lip hard. A lot of people, unfortunately, did care about things like that. "I went there because my dad did. Because that was the plan. I just followed along. Going to a good school doesn't make me smarter or better or anything." Frustrated, I raked my hand through my hair, tugging on it and welcoming the tiny bloom of pain. I didn't know what to say or how to say it. I glanced around Matt's cabin, my gaze coming to rest on the large windows. It was dark out but not quite night. Everything was cast in shades of evening blue: the stirring trees, the neat fields, the distant mountains.

"This—" I swept my hand around his home and toward the view. "—you should be proud of this. You're happy here, right?"

Matt deflated and sighed, dragging a hand over his face. "Yeah," he ground out. "I never thought I'd have anything this... healthy. I am proud of the farm. We worked hard to build this. Don't know about happy, though. Content for sure." Matt shrugged and turned toward the sink to start doing the dishes.

I eased the soapy sponge from his hand and bumped my hip against his. Thankfully he didn't argue when I started scrubbing the pans from dinner. "Hey, if you're not happy here, you could totally come to New York with me," I teased as I stacked dripping plates in the wooden drying rack laid out on a towel next to the sink.

Thankfully, Matt rewarded my pathetic effort to lighten the mood with a smirk. "Think I'd stick out?"

"Everyone fits in New York. But you might stand out because you're so gorgeous." I shrugged. I couldn't help but smile at the image of Matt, tall and broad in a flannel shirt and work boots, navigating the tourist-clogged streets of lower Manhattan, apologizing quietly and smirking as he ducked selfie-sticks and skirted around bedsheets laid out to display knock-off designer bags.

Matt scoffed and rolled his eyes, his demeanor settling back to his usual calm. I wasn't joking about him being gorgeous, though. One glance into his intense blue eyes or one flash of his surprisingly sweet smile and I melted. I craved the taste of his mouth and that low, possessive growl that rumbled through him each time our lips met. But there was no denying this was far more than sexual infatuation. My attraction to Matt was elemental. With him, I was at peace. Even tonight's heavier conversation felt safe. His sturdy quiet grounded me, leached away my unease and undid me. Although I sensed Matt was holding some of his emotions back—and I certainly didn't know how to unravel the knotted mess of feelings writhing inside me—I was filled with the blood-deep conviction that we fit together.

"Did you hear anything I said?" Matt asked without ire, tapping me gently on the forehead. He was once again busy at the stove, tipping spices into a small pot of something that smelled like comfort itself.

"Umm…."

Matt kissed me, and his mouth tasted like sweet apples and winter spices. "I asked you about the song you played last night."

My ears heated. Playing for Matt the night before, the music flowed through me, warm and bright, in a way it rarely did. I hadn't wanted to stop playing. I'd started piano lessons in preschool. And for years I'd fretted through performances for music teachers and crowds of high-achieving, competitive peers, and through long hours perfecting pieces, laboring over tiny flaws and tugging at my hair when a composition felt slightly off. After I'd been passed over for the conservatory spot, sometimes, sitting down in front of the piano, my fingers refused to move and my palms got sweaty. But they hadn't last night.

Matt laughed, and I buried my face in my hands. Yet again, I'd spaced out. "Fuck, I'm sorry," I grumbled. "But, yeah, the song I played was Tchaikovsky—the 'Waltz of the Flowers' from *The Nutcracker*. Did you like it?"

"Yup," Matt said softly as he tipped amber liquid into two mugs. "Never heard it before."

I tried not to let surprise show on my face. My mom was a season ticket holder at the New York City Ballet, and we'd seen *The Nutcracker* so many times

I could probably play the entire score in my sleep. It seemed strange to me that Matt could be unfamiliar with such a famous piece of music.

"Here." I hurried over to Matt's stereo system, eager to share this with him. "Is there an aux input? I have it in my music library. If you want, we can listen to the whole ballet."

A moment later we settled on the couch, a plate of chocolate chip cookies and two steaming mugs of cider on the coffee table in front of us. Biting into a cookie, I groaned as the crisp exterior gave way to a buttery sweet center, still a little warm. Matt looked undeniably pleased as I devoured the thing in two bites. I leaned into him with a small, contented sigh. The living room was dim, illuminated only by the shifting golden glow of the fire and the white strings of light on the tree. Moose, realizing we were not going to share anything with him, curled his giant brown-and-black body into a loop in front of the woodstove. The delicate notes of the overture floated around us, drifting through the air like snow. I looked again and again at the Christmas tree, the lights twinkling on the deep green boughs. Outside a wash of stars shone in the sky, sharp and clear white against the inky dark. I closed my eyes, desperate to sear every detail into my memory, knowing I would spend the rest of my life pining for this moment.

"You falling asleep, baby?" Matt drew me closer, his arms wrapping tighter around me, heavy and warm like a blanket. Shaking my head, I relaxed into him and breathed his smell.

"No," I murmured against the soft fabric of Matt's shirt, "I'm just really happy."

"Me too," he said softly. And his kiss felt like home.

Chapter Eleven

Mikah

THE mountaintops were chalk-white, so clear against the sky, it seemed like I could reach out and touch them. The sky out here was bigger, wider. I liked how it made me feel small. The snow had stopped this morning, but the air still smelled like it, fragile and clean. Gently, I ran my fingers over the coarse hair of the horse's mane. When Matt had suggested we go horseback riding, I'd completely failed to hide my horror. I'd never actually been on a horse, only seen them miserably pulling tourists around the city or kicking at the dirt paths in Central Park as the cops riding them blandly surveyed throngs of joggers and nannies with expensive strollers.

When Matt led me to the barn to formally introduce me to the farm's two horses, he informed me I would be riding the smaller one, a speckled mare named Nugget. Apparently she'd been christened by Abby, named after the eight-year-old's favorite food. The name fit too, because all Nugget seemed to want to do was eat any available thing we happened to pass as we rode along the snow-blanketed trails. Matt's giant brown horse, Memphis, was a far better listener, sticking to the path and keeping an even pace. Okay, Matt was also, unsurprisingly, excellent at controlling the animal with gentle movements and soft sounds of encouragement.

I muttered to myself as, once again, Nugget stalled to nibble at some scrubby underbrush. Could horses even eat that stuff? Was I about to let Matt's horse poison herself? Tugging on the reins the way Matt had shown me was fruitless. Nugget remained rooted to the spot, content to munch away at sharp, probably toxic foliage.

"You all right?" Matt turned his horse around, looking far too at ease and far too amused by my predicament.

"Can she eat this?" My voice sounded tinny and shrill, more panicked than I needed to be. I willed myself to calm the hell down.

"Yup. She's greedy, though, so don't let her eat too much." Matt made a quiet clicking sound, and Nugget turned immediately toward him. Traitor.

Without further incident I followed Matt through the snowy field, grateful for the warmth of my new coat as a huge gust of wind whipped across the open plain. Although the black work jacket wasn't the kind of clothing I usually gravitated to, I loved its comfortable practicality. Glancing up from my white-knuckled grip on the reins, I couldn't suppress an actual

sigh of awe. This place was breathtakingly beautiful.
The sun glittered on the freshly fallen snow, making
everything look bright and clean. And Matt looked
as gorgeous as the landscape around us, rugged and
natural, his thick thighs flexing as he easily controlled
the horse. I grinned to myself. Never would I have
imagined I would actually enjoy tromping over the
frozen ground on horseback, surrounded by nothing
but trees and mountains. I was at ease here. Whether it
was the holiday season, the whole splendor-of-nature
thing, the satisfaction of spending time with Matt, or a
combination of all three, I couldn't say.

Not for the first time, I wondered what it would be
like to actually live in a place like this. There was no
denying that the Teton Valley was beautiful. And the two
towns closest to Matt's farm seemed pretty cool, with
eclectic restaurants, an actual drive-in movie theater,
and a smattering of independently owned shops. The
tiny idealistic part of me loved imagining a life out here
with Matt: stargazing, hiking with Moose, learning how
to grow vegetables, waking up each morning wrapped
safe in his strong arms. But the bigger part of me knew
I was being ridiculous. For one, I had only known Matt
for a little over a month. Of course I liked everything
about him. We were firmly in the infatuation, can't-
keep-our-hands-off-each-other phase. It was idiotic for
me to think about living with him when I didn't even
know his middle name, not to mention actual important
things like if he wanted a long-term serious relationship
or how he navigated difficult arguments. He could be a
Republican for all I knew.

Really, all this nature stuff and relaxation was fine
and good for a few weeks, but I knew soon enough
I would start missing decent coffee shops and the

comfort of progressive urban spaces. Matt seemed pretty comfortable being out within his community, but he was also six foot five and built like a tank. It seemed highly unlikely that any bigoted assholes would be foolish enough to mess with him. But I wasn't particularly big or butch, and I certainly had zero interest in dealing with small-town homophobia. When I'd asked Matt about any local LGBTQ spaces or queer groups, he just shrugged and said he wasn't aware of anything like that. Back in Boston I'd been actively involved in a queer book club, sponsored my school's gay-straight alliance, and had volunteered at a LGBTQ youth center throughout college and grad school. I couldn't imagine the isolation of, quite literally, being the odd man out.

"Uncle Matt!" A small girl who had to be Abby bounded through the field in our direction, closely followed by Moose. Her shiny silver parka caught the sun, making me want to shield my eyes. The metallic coat paired with electric blue snow pants and a lime-green knit hat brought a smile to my face. Clearly this kid loved color.

"Hey, bug." Matt slid off Memphis easily and ruffled his niece's hat.

I wanted to follow Matt's lead, effortlessly dismounting the horse and saying hello, but I envisioned myself falling to the ground in a heap, so I settled for an awkward wave.

"Is this your boyfriend?" Abby asked, looking at me with wide eyes.

"This is my friend, Mikah." Matt didn't miss a beat, extending a hand to help me down off the horse. "Mikah, this is my niece, Abby."

Happy to be back on solid ground, I shook Abby's tiny, gloved hand. "Nice to meet you." I grinned at her. She was an adorable kid. "So is Nugget your horse?"

Abby nodded absently, her dark eyes plainly sizing me up. I felt myself trying to stand up a little taller. "Daddy said you're Uncle Matt's boyfriend. That's different from a friend. Boyfriend means you kiss."

Matt laughed, hurriedly stripping off his deerskin gloves and rummaging around in his pockets while I searched my mind for an appropriate response. *Oh yeah, Abby, well, I'm kind of falling for your uncle, but I also live on the East Coast, so we're keeping things casual. And we kiss all the time, and it's basically the greatest thing ever.* Definitely no good.

"I found this for you yesterday." Matt handed Abby the small piece of quartz he'd picked up while he and I had taken Moose for a walk along the Snake River.

Abby's eyes went wide as she looked down at the stone, awkward question thankfully forgotten. "A diamond?" She breathed the words.

"Umm," Matt hedged, trying not to smile, "you think?"

She bobbed her head sagely. "Yeah, the rock book says that diamonds are a very hard clear stone." She said the words like she was reading them directly from the page.

I bent down to inspect the rock, my face a mask of seriousness. "Well, this does appear to fit that description."

"What other kinds of rocks are clear?" Matt asked pointedly. Man, he could have been a teacher.

Abby considered his question. "Um… moonstone. Sometimes topaz. Oh! Quartz!" She beamed at him and pocketed the rock. Matt held out his hand for a fist bump. I tried not to die on the spot from the cuteness.

"So what're you up to out here?" Matt asked Abby as he gathered up the reins of both horses and started back in the direction of the barn. For that, I was thankful. Although my new coat was delightfully cozy, all of Matt's gloves had been way too big for me, so my hands were freezing. Plus, I could only stare at Matt's ass in those worn jeans for so long without wanting to drag him back to his cabin and pull said jeans off him. Nope, not thinking about that while in the presence of a child.

"Oh, yeah, I forgot. Mom wanted me to tell you that she made hot chocolate and that she wants you to come over for some."

I followed Matt and Abby into the barn, which unfortunately was so drafty that it wasn't much better than the windblown fields visible through the weathered wooden slats. Hot chocolate sounded amazing at the moment. Honestly, though, I'd rather have it in bed with Matt than with Matt's whole family, not that they didn't seem like lovely people. I watched uselessly as Matt made quick work of removing the horses' heavy saddles and hanging them on rough-hewn posts. Abby grabbed a small brush and started running it over Nugget's speckled body, petting the horse and talking to her in a gentle voice.

"Um, can I help at all?" I asked, weirdly embarrassed that I was so out of my depth.

Matt nodded in the direction of a cement utility sink. "You can refill their water if you want. What's in there might be frozen. Abby and I can take care of the rest."

I wanted to grumble that I could handle the same tasks as a second grader, but truthfully Abby had moved on to doing something to the horse's hooves, and I wasn't so sure. By the time I lugged a bucket of water to the trough, both horses were happily munching on hay in their stalls.

"What do you say, Mikah? Want some hot chocolate?" My stomach fluttered at the heat in Matt's gaze. I knew what he wanted to do, and it didn't involve going over to his brother's place.

"Please! Please!" Abby grabbed my hand. "I want to show Mikah my geology kit. Oh, and we can do beads."

"Hot chocolate sounds good." I tried to match Abby's enthusiasm as Matt closed the barn door behind us. Our other plans could wait.

Abby and Moose bounded ahead in the direction of the modest, brightly decorated split-level ranch. Once his niece was a good distance away, waving a stick in front of Moose's face, Matt pulled me to him, kissing me rough and fast. My skin flushed with arousal, and I wrapped my arms around his waist. When my hands drifted lower to squeeze Matt's thighs, he groaned and pushed his face into my hair.

"You like that, huh?" I teased, tipping my face back and swiping a quick kiss over his cold lips.

"Yup." Matt's voice was a husky whisper as he rocked his hips against mine, showing me exactly how much he liked my hands on him.

"Behave." I kissed his stubbly cheek before giving it a gentle pat. "I don't really want to have a boner when I meet your brother this time."

THE interior of John and Katie's house was the polar opposite of Matt's cabin. Where Matt's place was comfortable in its simplicity, his brother's house exploded with color and clutter. There were toys, framed photos, and little decorative signs everywhere. The place was nice, though, if a little overwhelming.

"You found 'em?" Matt's sister-in-law called from the kitchen as we pulled off our boots and hung our coats on an overburdened rack. I liked the sound of her voice, musical and low with a slight country accent.

"Uh-huh!" Abby shouted back, galloping into the kitchen. Beneath the colorful winter gear, she wore an even brighter pair of leggings printed with gumdrops.

My heart rate picked up as I followed Matt into the kitchen. John, a slightly shorter, darker-haired version of Matt, and his wife were busy putting together what appeared to be a cookie tray for fifty people.

"Hey, Mikah!" John pulled me into a bear hug. "Good to see you again, dude!" I found myself smiling despite the fact that I wasn't much of a hugger when it came to people I didn't know very well. Matt's brother was the kind of person you couldn't help but like, though, with his easy manner and, evidently, free-flowing affection. I was glad Matt had such loving people in his life.

Matt's sister-in-law grinned at me. "So nice to finally meet you. I'm Katie." She wiped her hands on a gingham kitchen towel before shaking mine.

"Thanks for having us over," I mumbled. I felt a little awkward getting to know Matt's family. Sure, he'd met my family too, but this all felt very… intimate. Like an actual relationship. It was getting harder and harder to convince myself that this bore any resemblance to a casual holiday fling.

"What's all this?" Matt asked, gesturing to the cookies and steaming mugs of hot chocolate. The whole display looked like something out of a food magazine, each cup topped with a swirl of whipped cream and a dusting of crushed candy cane.

"We wanted to pull out all the stops for your boyfriend." John picked up the tray and gestured for us to follow him to the kitchen table.

"John...." Katie chastised him.

My head spun. Was Matt calling me his boyfriend? A quick glance in his direction answered the question for me, however. Matt was rubbing his neck, something I'd come to recognize as a clear sign of his discomfort, and staring daggers at his brother.

"Oh, sorry, 'friend,'" John amended, putting scare quotes around the last word.

I was grateful when Katie, with an admirable level of tact, changed the topic to horseback riding, asking Matt and me lighthearted questions about the weather and where we'd gone. I liked seeing Matt with his family. He was still reserved, still kept his responses short and simple, but he was animated. His enthusiastic gestures and easy laugh warmed me all the way through.

"So what do you do, Mikah?" Katie's question startled me. I'd zoned out of the conversation, which had shifted from horseback riding to something farm-related.

"I'm a teacher. Well, I used to be." Could I still call myself an educator even though I was currently doing nothing but reading, messing around on the piano, and letting myself get way too invested in a man who lived thousands of miles away from me?

"That's awesome! Me too!" Katie clapped her hands. I could tell she was probably an amazing teacher, the kind of organized, peppy instructor who got kids excited with games and creative lesson plans. "What subject?"

I told her about my short-lived career with Boston Public Schools and about my upcoming interview at Walton, leaving out my misgivings about returning to the same elite school I'd attended for most of my life.

"Darn. Too bad you're not sticking around here," Katie mused, biting into a gingerbread cookie. Matt glanced over at me for a moment, then rubbed the back of his neck and became very interested in a loose thread on the red-and-green plaid placemat in front of him. "Maureen Thomas, the ninth-grade English teacher, announced at the holiday party that she's going to retire at the end of the year. She's amazing, really clicks with the kids and gets them interested in reading. It's always cool for me because they connect things from the novels to social studies. Hooray for interdisciplinary crossover!" She punched the air, and her husband chuckled fondly. "Anyway," Katie continued, "it'll be hard to replace her. I'm the team leader for ninth grade, and it was impossible to find a good fit when the Physical Science teacher quit last year. So many people come and go around here...." She shrugged and waved her hand toward the door.

My stomach flipped at her words. If a perfect solution existed, this was it. I could tell Matt was as aware as I was of the implications of what Katie said. Next to me, Matt's leg bounced rapid-fire under the table. I could stay. I could apply for the job here and... what? Live with Matt? Stay at my dad's place? Find an apartment in town? I tried to reel in my rapidly unspooling thoughts, but it was no use. The possibility of building something real and lasting with Matt dangled in front of me, alluring but somehow just out of reach.

An awkward silence settled over the table, only interrupted by the sound of Abby playing with action figures in the living room. I took a long sip of my hot chocolate, searching for any good small-talk topics to dispel the low-grade tingle of discomfort at the table.

John beat me to it, though, clearing his throat and asking about plans for New Year's Eve. Matt shook his head, slightly guarded as he turned toward me.

I perked up. Following my parents' divorce when I was in high school, my dad had started throwing a huge New Year's Eve party every year, first at his place in the Hollywood Hills and later at his house in Jackson Hole. I was pretty sure, in fact, that he'd met Naomi at one of his wilder soirees. The parties were always elaborate, elegant affairs complete with catered food, live music, and lots of rich lawyers getting wasted on champagne.

"My dad's having a big party," I blurted out. "At his house. You guys should all come. It'll be fun. I guess my stepmom is obsessed with New Year's, and she's been working superhard to make it nice."

"Okay," Matt said simply, putting his hand over mine on the table. I shivered as the warmth of his touch seemed to seep up my arm.

"Yes!" Katie beamed at John, who did not look nearly as excited by the offer. Before he could voice his hesitation, however, she'd pulled her phone from her pocket, her fingers flying over the screen. "John, don't you dare say no. We haven't had a date night in about four months. And what's more romantic than a New Year's party? Sure beats me cooking dinner, doing the dishes, and watching the ball drop by myself while you and Abby conk out on the sofa." Katie winked at me. A moment later her phone buzzed and she flashed a thumbs-up. "Perfect, Bella said she's free that night to watch Abby."

A series of cheers about pizza and freeze dance issued from the other room. Clearly Abby had been listening in on our conversation.

Katie rose from the table, kissing the top of John's head. The guy looked torn between irritation and amusement. "Thanks a lot, man." John laughed, shaking his head at me. "Now I gotta find some fancy stuff to wear."

I waved my hands. "No way! It's, like, business casual or whatever. Don't worry about it. My dad always pulls out all the stops, but seriously wear whatever you want."

"Oh yes way. We're dressing up," Katie called from the kitchen, her voice lethal.

John groaned. "She gonna make me wear a dang tie… I just know it."

THE sun dipped behind the mist-cloaked mountains, painting the sky a hazy pink as I followed Matt back to his cabin. It had gotten even colder when the clouds rolled in, and I couldn't wait to relax in front of the fire with Matt. Preferably naked, with his rough hands rendering me feverish with pleasure. As we drew closer to Matt's house, my phone connected to his Wi-Fi, buzzing in my pocket with a text from Elena. I shouldn't have been surprised that my sister was asking if I planned to ever come back to our dad's place. I'd spent three of the four nights since Christmas at Matt's cabin. He'd taken me to dinner at an adorably cozy restaurant in town, which I'd loved. And he'd taken me backcountry skiing, which I'd hated. I did feel a little guilty for spending so much time away from my family. But not guilty enough to want to go back over to my dad's. Besides, I would be seeing a lot of Elena back in Manhattan, and my dad and Luca had spent every waking moment since Christmas holed up in my dad's office, catching up on work. Even Naomi had been putting in hectic hours at the yoga studio, busy with clients looking to center themselves after the holiday mayhem. I was so focused on rapid-fire tapping out a snarky response to my sister that I collided with Matt, who had stopped walking and was gazing out at the mountains. Quickly, I hit Send on the text and shoved my phone back in my pocket.

"Sorry," I murmured, but I wasn't really as Matt turned, holding me in his big arms and surrounding me with his body heat. He was always so solid and sure around me.

"I love watching the sun set." Matt's voice was soft, and I realized he was looking not at the dusky ribbons of rose and gold on the horizon but down at me.

My breath caught in my throat. I hadn't anticipated what hearing the word *love* in Matt's low, husky voice would do to me. I wanted all of that affection for myself. I twined my arms around his neck. We stood together for a long while, just breathing and watching as the sun dipped behind the mountains and the shadows stretched out long on the snow.

When Matt looked down at me, his eyebrows knitted together, I worried he was about to bring up the job thing—the question of me leaving, the prospect of me staying, the chance that this could become something real. I didn't know what to feel about it, much less what to say. Smoothing my fingertips over his face to relax his features had its intended effect:

Matt smiled shyly and grazed my lips with his. I had never been with someone who liked kissing as much as Matt. Not that I was complaining; I couldn't get enough of the feeling of his mouth on mine, simultaneously possessive and tender.

"Do you have to go home?" he asked, turning back in the direction of his cabin. Even with the windows dark, the place was inviting, blanketed in clean white snow and surrounded by frosty evergreens. I couldn't wait to get inside.

"No. Unless you want some time to yourself tonight? No worries if you do." I dreaded the prospect of falling asleep alone, but I also didn't want to be the clingy weirdo who ignored social cues and overstayed his welcome. The fear of being honest about what I actually wanted was hard to shake.

"Mikah." Matt sounded almost stern, and damn, if it didn't turn me on a little. "You know I want you to stay."

I grinned, relief unwinding the tight fibers of my muscles, although part of me wondered if this conversation had taken on a larger significance. "Okay. Then I'll cook for you. If the grocery store's still open, I can make you *anelletti al forno*, although I doubt they'll have the right kind of pasta…. I could probably get away with ditalini if they have those." I was rambling, but Matt didn't seem to care.

"I like when you speak Italian." His voice dipped low and heat pooled in my groin.

"*Davvero*?" I teased, rolling my r's exaggeratedly. "I'll have to keep that in mind." I wasn't opposed to doing a little bilingual dirty talk in bed.

Matt grabbed my hand, tugging me up the stairs to his cabin. It was undeniable that I was letting myself fall in too deep with Matt. But I had no desire to pull away. Because I knew this was it. This was the kind of relationship I'd scrambled to build with guys like Josh who were more interested in keeping their options open than investing in the person right in front of them. When I was with Matt, I could feel his care, bask in his affection, surround myself with his... love? Ugh, I needed to calm the hell down. I shook my head at my own stupidity. People didn't fall in love this quickly. There was no way what I was feeling was anything more than a heady crush. Matt was a practical, even-keeled guy. I doubted he had any misconceptions about what was going on between us.

The moment the front door clicked shut, Matt pushed me back against it, his thick arms framing my body. Everything between us was electric heat as our lips touched. Matt was rushed and eager, his movements a little clumsy. My head spun, but I was grateful for the distraction from my typical overthinking and brooding. Matt held me close, his breaths coming heavy, body warm against me. Sinking into the slick daze of lust, an unexpected laugh bubbled up from my chest. We probably weren't going to make it to the grocery store.

Chapter Twelve

Matt

"HOLY fucking shit, bro. Your boyfriend is loaded."
John's face was the picture of disbelief as we pulled up
to the Cerullos' giant house.

"Jonathan Haskell! Watch your language." Katie
swatted his arm.

I said nothing. I'd definitely been surprised when
I pulled up to the expansive log-and-stone mansion on
Christmas Eve, so I really couldn't imagine how John
and Katie were feeling now. The well-maintained trees
around the house were tastefully uplit, and the wide
brick driveway was packed with luxury cars. As we
drew closer to the house, a young woman in a red parka
jogged over. She gestured for John to roll down the

window of his truck. A hot flare of uncertainty had me pressing my lips together, wondering if she was going to ask us to show some kind of invitation.

"Good evening," she chirped. "I'm happy to park the car for you if you folks want to head inside."

John grumbled something about being able to park his own damn truck but handed over his keys. As much as I wanted to see Mikah, part of me regretted agreeing to come to this party. John didn't have a whole lot of patience for the rich vacation-home crowd, and I didn't have a whole lot of patience for crowds, period. I tugged at the hem of my sweater as we walked up the pathway to the house. The flagstones were cleared of snow and flanked with what appeared to be flickering candles in decorative white and silver bags.

As John, Katie, and I had clambered into his truck to head over to the party, I'd insisted the event wasn't going to be all that fancy. Sure, Mikah's family was rich, but Christmas Eve had been a casual, cozy night. The focus had been on the food and enjoying each other's company. Clearly I had been wrong. Ahead of us a pair of women in impossibly high heels and slinky black dresses giggled as they picked their way up the stairs to the door. My heavy cream-colored cable-knit sweater and the nicest pair of jeans I owned were probably going to stick out a little bit. At least John and Katie looked classy. Katie wore a pretty blue velvet dress, and John had reluctantly put on the khakis and a black button-down his wife had picked out for him.

John continued to curse under his breath as we walked through the open door. The floral arrangements had been updated. Gone were the red poinsettias and sprigs of pine and holly. We were greeted by a towering twist of white peonies and roses interspersed with silver twigs and birch branches in the center of the cavernous foyer. Clearly, Mikah's stepmom knew a great florist. Glancing around, I saw no sign of Mikah or any member of the Cerullo family, only throngs of strangers in dark suits and elegant dresses.

"Wow, Matt, this really is... something," Katie murmured, her eyes darting around just as mine had. I'd never heard her voice sound so small.

"Yup." I nodded, now desperate to find Mikah. Maybe we should head out? This wasn't our kind of party.

"Matt!" A high, clear voice rang out, and Elena poked her head around the archway leading to the kitchen. "Yay! Mikah was getting ready to text you." She barreled toward us, her baggy gray dress and long sweater a welcome sight. She wasn't even wearing shoes, just a pair of mismatched wool socks.

"Thanks for having us." I fell back on manners. "This is my brother, John, and my sister-in-law, Katie."

Before either of them could respond, Elena was kissing their cheeks and inviting them to follow her into the kitchen for a drink. Damn, she was such an easy person to like. As relieved as I was to see Elena, that didn't stop me from scanning the crowded kitchen for Mikah's smoldering brown eyes and mess of curls. People chatted amiably in groups of three or four, sipping champagne in tall flutes as jazz music filtered in from the living room. A few waiters in starched white shirts drifted around with tiny appetizers arranged on trays.

A heavy hand, too big to be Mikah's, grabbed my shoulder, and I turned to find Luca clutching a glass of red wine, his face impassive.

"Hey," I said, pushing down my desire to immediately ask where my... Mikah was.

"Good to see you, Matt. Mikah's around here somewhere. He couldn't wait for you to show up." Luca made it sound like a bad thing.

I nodded, glancing over at Elena, who had gotten John and Katie situated with food and drinks. The three of them were laughing. Figuring it would be rude to excuse myself back to more pleasant company, I turned my attention back to Mikah's older brother.

"You want something to drink, man? My dad pulled some of the Sassicaia out of the cellar. It's killer."

Having no idea what that was, but figuring it was wine, I shook my head. I wasn't exactly uncomfortable around Luca. And he didn't necessarily seem like a bad person, but something told me he had an issue with me.

His broad shoulders relaxed a little, and he scrubbed a hand over his beard. "Look, Matt, can I be honest with you?"

I thought the question was rhetorical, but Luca waited for me to nod before continuing.

"Mikah's an amazing kid. I mean he's my brother, so of course I love him. But he—" Luca smiled softly. "He's brilliant. And he cares a lot, you know? Even though he puts up a front and tries to act like stuff doesn't bother him. He's, well…." He pressed his lips together firmly, clearly weighing his words. "He's sensitive. And I think this year was tough on him. Not only with the job thing, but…. He just doesn't have the greatest self-esteem right now. And when Mikah actually lets himself feel something, he *feels it*, you know? So I'm worried about him with you. How he's going to handle you two splitting up when he goes back to New York. I can tell he likes you a lot." Luca's gaze fell on the necklace. I'd been messing with it in the car and had forgotten to tuck it under my sweater. Plus I'd kind of wanted Mikah to see how much I loved it. Now, though, I quickly hid it away under the knit fabric.

"Okay," I said simply after another long, uncomfortable pause. My mind was racing. Concern and a sharp pang of sadness warred with my desire to ask when exactly Mikah was going back. I knew it was a conversation we'd both been avoiding. My emotions weighed so heavily on my chest, I had to will myself to breathe.

Luca's face transformed, and he put up a hand. "Sorry to be so blunt," he hurried to say. "But I don't want to see him heartbroken. And honestly, I meant it when I said you seem like a good guy. I don't want you to get too wrapped up in this either."

It's a little late for that, I wanted to say, but instead I lifted a shoulder noncommittally. "I really care about Mikah. Distance isn't gonna change that."

Thin arms snaked around my waist, and Mikah's familiar citrusy smell washed over me. I couldn't help but grin. He looked adorable in a slightly rumpled white shirt untucked under yet another of his raggedy black sweaters. I would miss those ragtag things. He pressed his lips gently to mine, and I let my eyes drift shut, just for a moment. As much as kissing Mikah had quickly risen right to the top of the list of my favorite things in the world, I was still a little uncomfortable with the display of affection in such a crowded room. It was still a new thing for me to show affection in front of strangers. But if anyone cared that two men were kissing, they certainly weren't showing it. Not even Luca seemed bothered.

"Was my brother being weird?" Mikah directed the question at Luca instead of me.

Luca made a so-so gesture with his hand while I shook my head.

"Ugh. Luca, stop being the worst. Anyway, sorry it took me so long to find you." He kissed me again, grinning hugely. A genuine smile, warm and bright. I couldn't remember the last time someone had seemed so happy to see me. My face heated. "I got trapped in a conversation with some old dude complaining about how bad public schools are. Seriously, if I have to listen to another person who has spent literally *zero* time in a classroom, bitching about public education, I'm going to start screaming. Like actual full-blown yelling in public."

I laughed. "I always liked school." This was true. School had been a safe, structured place. A place where I could lose myself in numbers and solve problems that made sense.

"I knew I loved you." He squeezed my bicep playfully, but the words still hit my stomach like a huge gulp of something hot. "You want a beer or something? There's other stuff too, champagne, water, mocktails…." Mikah inclined his head vaguely in the direction of the living room.

"What the hell is a mocktail?" I asked, and both Mikah and Luca laughed.

I tried to follow what Mikah was saying about fresh fruit juices and herb infusions but was immediately overwhelmed by the crush of bodies as we wandered into what had once been the Cerullos' living room. The space was wholly transformed. The soft leather sofas and oatmeal-colored tufted armchairs were nowhere to be seen. In their place was a silver-and-white dance floor and a half-dozen spindly cocktail tables topped with candles and fresh flowers. Strings of white lights stretched overhead. A full bar was set up next to the roaring fire, and a live jazz trio played lively, unobtrusive music. It was strange seeing a woman with flowing gray hair, seated at the piano instead of Mikah, watching her hands rather than his as they slid over the black and white keys. I knew absolutely nothing about music, but I liked the way he played better. I was probably more than a little biased, though.

Most of the guests clung to the edges of the enormous living room, drinking and chatting, but a few older couples swept around the dance floor with confident, practiced movements. Almost everyone was dressed beautifully, in sharp, well-fitting suits and elegant dresses. Once again I tugged at my sweater, the wool feeling suddenly too hot and too rough against my skin.

"I kind of figured you might not be big on parties," Mikah said in my ear. I shivered at the brush of his breath over my skin.

"They're okay," I lied. I had never liked parties. Not the loud get-togethers my parents had occasionally hosted. Not the barn keggers filled with girls I disappointed and guys who chugged beer after beer, crushing the cans and tossing them aside. Not even fancy events like this. Although, aside from Katie and John's wedding, this was really the only party of the tiny-appetizer-and-wine-in-glasses variety I'd been to.

Mikah's fingers, so cold I startled at the touch, slipped under my sweater and massaged the bare skin of my lower back. I leaned into him the way Moose did when I scratched the right spot behind his ears. My whole body went slack. My weight was too much against Mikah's smaller frame, though, and we both stumbled. A giggle bubbled out of Mikah's throat as I braced a hand against the wall to keep us from falling. His eyes went wide, and I realized I was basically pinning him into the corner. But then he was kissing me, and all that mattered was the softness of his lips on mine and the feeling of his fingers, still gently kneading my skin.

"Whoa," Mikah sighed as he pulled back. He was grinning and blushing and looked so cute I never wanted to stop kissing him. "Okay, we can't keep doing *that* in this crowded-ass room. But, how about I entertain you with some gossip?" He laced his fingers with mine and pulled me to the bar, quickly grabbing us two glasses of champagne.

I couldn't help laughing. Mikah's frantic energy made everything fun. I loved how he bounced between driving me wild with gentle touches and searing kisses to cracking me up as he surreptitiously pointed out various women Luca had slept with. Apparently four of them were fitness models with huge Instagram followings. Really, though, I had no idea what a fitness model was, and farming forums were about as social-media savvy as I got.

"Okay…. So check out the guy talking to Naomi." He gestured slyly to a handsome black man wearing what looked like a very expensive dark blue suit. "That's Ken Ezekiel." Mikah said the name like it meant something big.

I shook my head.

"Sorry, I forget not everyone is a poetry fanboy like me." Mikah rolled his eyes at himself. "He's the editor-in-chief of *Incanto Magazine.* He used to teach writing at Harvard too. But of course he left right before I got there. I've probably read *Vermillion,* his first collection, about fifty times. Anyway, I guess he has a place out here, and he does yoga at Naomi's studio. They're, like, actual friends. Who knew Naomi was so cool? He came to Thanksgiving, and I was ridiculously nervous. I thought I was going to swallow my tongue. He's a supernice guy, though. He even offered to read my stuff… which, like, no way. That's too scary to even think about because my poetry is emo garbage."

I could have let jealousy swell big and toxic inside me. I could have worried that I was all wrong for Mikah.

I could have flushed with shame because I knew nothing about poetry other than the few fragments I remembered from English class. But more than anything else, I was eager to listen. I loved learning from Mikah. Loved the way his hands flew wildly when he got excited. Loved that his voice got clear and strong when he was talking about something that interested him. Loved the way his eyes went liquid and sleepy when we touched. I loved him. The words were in my mouth, and I liked the way they felt there. But I swallowed them down. Telling Mikah would only make things harder for both of us. Those words wouldn't make him stay. Wouldn't take away the hurt when he left.

I squeezed Mikah's shoulder. "Could I read it? Your writing, I mean."

"Maybe someday. If my stuff is ever decent." His tone was casual, but as he realized the implication of his words, his face crumpled. *Someday* wasn't happening. Mikah was leaving. We might exchange the occasional bland text every few weeks, nothing too personal, but those would get further and further apart. We'd disappear from each other's lives, fading to warm memories and nothing more.

I took a small sip of my champagne. I hardly ever drank aside from the occasional beer if I went out for a quick meal, but I knew I would never be able to touch champagne again. The soft, bright flavor would only remind me of Mikah.

Stefano and Naomi danced gracefully, holding each other close and moving slowly to the music. On the other side of the living room, Katie cajoled my brother to dance, his hands stuffed in his pockets while she tossed her head back in exasperation. They'd be dancing in no time, Katie beaming and John looking like he was stepping over broken glass instead of the polished surface of a temporary dance floor.

"Wanna dance?" I asked. The look of genuine surprise that blossomed on Mikah's face was more than worth the awkwardness of my terrible dancing.

"I wasn't even going to ask. I figured you'd be like 'Nope. Don't dance.'" He dropped his voice low and squinted his eyes like a cowboy in a spaghetti western.

"Are you mocking me?"

"Yup." Mikah hooked his thumbs in his belt loops, apparently still intent on impersonating me.

"Come on." I set our glasses down on the bar. Then we were on the dance floor, and Mikah was in my arms. I tapped my forehead to his.

All around us couples drifted and swayed in time with the music. Glasses tinkled, and the lights above us cast everything in a silvery shimmer. I nodded at my brother, who had indeed been wheedled into dancing and was shifting from foot to foot, each movement out of sync with the swinging beat. Katie looked thrilled nonetheless, her arms looped around his neck, dark hair gleaming down her back in pretty waves. Through the mass of partygoers, I stared out the window at fat snowflakes catching and twisting in the wind outside.

Mikah was compact and perfect in my arms, clinging to me like a lichen on a tree trunk. He was beautiful in the twinkling light as he dropped his head to my shoulder. A new song started, and I took both of his hands in mine. Joy welled up in my chest, spreading to fill my body. I felt buoyant. Distantly I heard someone yell, "Twenty minutes till midnight!" I let go of Mikah's hands and drew him into a tight hug. My breaths came steady and slow. We weren't really dancing anymore, just standing on the dance floor holding each other. But I needed him close. Needed him with me.

Chapter Thirteen

Mikah

WHEN the jazz trio started playing the slippery notes of "Moonlight Serenade," I snorted. I hated this song. Really, I had never been much of a Glenn Miller fan. I basically saw him as the fast food of composers, enjoyable but ultimately too generic to be truly satisfying. But, damn, if my eyes didn't blur with tears when, as the music rose, I caught a glimpse of Matt's and my reflection in the snowy, dark window, his cream sweater standing out among the sea of black formalwear. We swayed slowly, his arms tight around me, his big body relaxed into mine. We looked happy. And now I knew I was going to cry every time I heard this stupid song.

"What's so funny?" Matt tipped my face up to his.

I hiccupped a half laugh, half sob. The lights overhead sparkled through the blur of my tears. My heartbeat felt strange, like it raced hard against my rib cage and slowed to a crawl and then raced again. My emotions were all mixed up. I was fizzy with happiness, drifting along the rolling notes of the music. I was almost stepping on Matt's heavy boots in an effort to stay as close to him as possible. Never in my life had I felt so simultaneously content and desperately terrified. The mess of feelings overwhelmed me, making my lips form the words before I could overthink them.

"I'm pretty sure I'm kind of in love with you. I get that it probably sounds ridiculous since we, like, barely know each other. But... yeah." I was talking fast, the confession coming out a blurred mess.

Matt froze. The couples around us kept giggling and sipping champagne. The music played on. A peal of laughter floated in from the kitchen. A heavy gust of wind rattled the windows. Then I was in Matt's powerful arms as he lifted me against him, quite literally sweeping me off my feet. He squeezed me tight, and his mouth claimed mine. Laughter rumbled through him. I grinned against his lips. Next to us someone whooped. Matt and I laughed harder.

"Kind of?" Matt shook his head, still grinning.

My face was glowing hot. I groaned and squeezed my eyes shut, suddenly unable to speak.

"I love you, Mikah. So much." He kissed my forehead and set me gently back on my feet.

I took a deep, slow breath and made myself look directly into Matt's summer-sky eyes. "And I'm going back to New York in three days. On Thursday. I have that job interview, and it kind of seems like a sure thing… so." I couldn't help the giggle that escaped my lips. "Now what do we do?"

Matt's lips were so soft as he spoke into my mouth. "I don't know."

The air between us snapped clear and bright, like a cold wind had cleared away any remaining hesitation. Being in love didn't change reality. It didn't mean I would magically decide to throw away the opportunity at Walton. It didn't mean Matt would suddenly decide to leave the farm he'd spent over a decade building. But it did mean that I felt warm and safe and seen. That Matt knew how deeply I cared for him. That I had given voice to a feeling that I knew was right. And that was enough for now. It had to be.

Dimly, I was aware of the people around us counting down from ten, the rhythmic chant of numbers rising over the music. I pressed up on the balls of my feet to graze my lips over Matt's as confetti swirled down around us. A surging swell of "Happy New Year!" and those horrible noisemakers Elena insisted on buying filled the room. Time was a strange thing. The last month and a half had flown by. I was confident, however, that this upcoming year in New York, falling asleep without Matt, getting teary-eyed whenever I heard Elvis, would be a long and lonely one.

Matt smiled into the kiss, dragging his lips to my ear. "Happy New Year." His voice was husky and sent a delicious shiver rippling over my skin.

I closed my eyes and pressed my face into the rough fabric of his sweater, trying and failing to hold back a yawn. I was suddenly exhausted, drained from the emotional marathon I insisted on putting myself through. All I wanted was to curl up in bed with Matt, to fall asleep surrounded by his big body and even breaths.

"Tired?" Matt sifted his fingers through my hair, gently lifting my face so he could look into my eyes.

I nodded. "Will you stay?"

His face went serious, his expression shifting from tender to sad for just a moment. Then he grinned and disappeared into the sea of bodies to say good night to his brother and sister-in-law.

ALL traces of my earlier sleepiness had evaporated as I stood next to Matt in the harshly lit bathroom. Making occasional eye contact in the mirror, we brushed our teeth and washed up for bed. Matt had shed his sweater and jeans and laughed when he caught me ogling his reflection. I was a little worried he might tease me about the elaborate nature of my skincare routine, since the nights I'd slept over at his place I'd opted to leave my toiletry bag and six-step system at home. As I patted my cheeks with a vitamin C serum, however, Matt sheepishly asked if he could use some. Then all bets were off, and I spent a solid ten minutes talking him through the importance of night moisturizers and daily sunscreen. For someone who spent almost all of his time outside in harsh wind and glaring sun, he didn't seem particularly concerned about the risks the elements posed to his beautiful face.

"Well, at least promise me you'll start wearing sunscreen every day."

Matt's eyebrows drew together. He looked genuinely confused. "In the winter? I mean, in summer I wear a hat."

"All year. Every. Single. Day." I annunciated each word carefully. "I don't want you getting skin cancer." I kissed the corner of his mouth, which was sweet and minty from the toothpaste.

"Okay." He shrugged. "I promise."

"I'm holding you to it." My smile was forced as I flipped off the bathroom light and padded over to my bed. What, was I going to text him to check that he was taking care of his skin? *Hey, it's me, the guy who fell in love with you and then bailed like a total asshole. Hope you put some SPF 25 on this morning!*

Matt had, of course, lit a fire in the hearth the moment we undressed and he noticed I was shivering. I neglected to tell him my trembling had far more to do with the feelings clawing at my gut than the chill in the air. Now, though, the soothing, earthy smell of woodsmoke and the soft crackle of flames filled my bedroom. The party was still in full swing. The jazz trio and a good chunk of my dad's business associates had left shortly after midnight. Now the heavy thump of pop music and the odd, drunken shriek occasionally pierced the quiet enveloping us as we slid between the sheets.

I wanted Matt to fall asleep right away. I wanted to lie next to him in the dark and do nothing more than memorize the cadence of his breathing. I wanted everything to be peaceful and easy. I didn't want to do the big what-does-this-all-mean talk. I didn't have any answers, and I knew Matt didn't either.

We did spend the whole night talking. But, for once, I didn't overanalyze or shut down. We just talked. Never had I enjoyed the hours between midnight and sunrise so much. We talked about stupid stuff: TV shows we watched as kids, favorite foods, awkward date stories.

I learned that Matt had watched hours of late-night *Brady Bunch* reruns and had been heartbreakingly jealous of the fake family's pleasantly chaotic suburban life. Laughing at himself, he told me about his intense childhood crush on one of his brother's 4-H buddies, a guy who went by Bud and apparently had the same soulful eyes as Elvis. Matt loved desserts with cinnamon and had never tried sushi. He blushed to his ears in the dim firelight when he told how lucky he felt to go on actual dates with me. That he'd always hooked up with the occasional tourist and a few closeted guys he knew from growing up. I learned that his middle name was James, and that he, thankfully, was not a Republican.

We delved into heavier things too: how we first became aware of our own queerness, how badly Matt wanted a family but was pretty sure it would never work out for him, how the idea of letting someone really get to know me made my stomach pinch with fear. His voice was so distant when he talked about wanting kids that I pulled him close and held him for a long time. I couldn't tell him it was something I wanted too, knowing the admission would just add another layer of difficulty to this whole thing. I could taste an edge of salt on his lips and felt dampness on his cheeks as he held me close when I told him how safe I felt with him, how he made the world seem like a calmer, better place.

Matt drifted off around dawn, his face relaxed and bathed in diffuse gray morning light. I didn't sleep at all.

EVERYTHING around us was chaotic movement. In the front seat of his truck, though, Matt and I were motionless. Cars honked. People fumbled with tickets and luggage. A short man with a bushy beard hugged a young woman goodbye. He waved as she tugged her rolling suitcase through the sliding automatic doors and kept waving as she disappeared into the airport. Behind the low-slung building, the snowy peaks of the Tetons rose against a cloudless sky. We were as silent as the mountains. We'd been sitting here for twenty-seven minutes, not speaking, not getting out of the car, not even unbuckling our seat belts. My flight boarded in a half hour.

"Well." Matt rubbed his hands on his jeans and glanced at the green digital numbers on the dashboard clock. "You better go in, huh?"

I nodded but still didn't move. My throat tightened and my nose itched. I pressed my lips together. It was my nonna's voice in my head, lilting and soft, that jolted me into motion. *Breathe, caro.* So I did. Then I turned to Matt, trying for a smile that probably came out looking like a grimace. He was gripping his knees hard, his lips pressed so firmly together they were almost white.

"I'll be back in June." My voice sounded weird, fake and way too bright. "I'm flying back to get my car so I can drive it back to New York once I have a place. We'll talk. Stay friends, right?" My voice cracked on the last word. Acting like leaving the man I loved was no big deal made me feel shaky and hot. I worried I might actually throw up.

Matt shrugged and unbuckled his seat belt. I couldn't tell if he was angry. He certainly didn't meet my eye as he lifted my suitcases out of the bed of the truck and lined them up neatly on the curb.

"Okay, well, uh, I'll text you when I land." The need to press my face against Matt's chest, to inhale his

clean pine smell, to wrap myself in his quiet stability
was overwhelming. But at the same time, everything
was starting to feel foggy and detached. My gaze
pinged wildly, from Matt to the airport to the little girl
trying to balance her teddy bear on the handle of her
tiny purple suitcase. My thoughts were a tangled blur,
moving so quickly, I couldn't seem to grab on to one.
I needed to get on the plane before I started publicly
weeping.

Then Matt pulled me into his arms, gripping the
back of the coat he'd given me. He hugged me exactly
as tight as I needed. That weird homesick feeling
twisted through me. The wind was bitterly cold against
the tears sliding down my cheeks. My eyes fluttered
closed as I melted against his broad, sturdy frame. I
could feel Matt's chest rising and falling fast. He kissed
the side of my head, resting his lips against my hair.
He held me for a long time. A plane roared above us. I
wished it was mine, leaving without me. It wasn't.

Matt moved his hands to my shoulders, squeezing
them gently as he stared into my eyes. His blue eyes
were too intent, too pleading. My gaze crashed to the
ground. Our feet were so close together, I was almost
stepping on his boots. "Please stay." His voice was low
and rough.

"I can't." I pulled into myself as my heart broke.

Matt's eyes asked why, but his lips remained firmly
pressed together.

I wanted to tell him why I was leaving: *because
you're all I want and I'm terrified, because I need you
but I'm too afraid to take what I need, because I'm a
coward.* Instead my silence left me feeling like I was
scrambling to pick up the pieces of myself as the wind
whipped them away.

My mouth was thick with fear. I was really about to do this. I was about to leave the only man I'd ever truly loved. This wasn't a movie airport scene. Matt wasn't the type to run out onto the tarmac. And I was too worn out to even think about springing up out of my tiny airplane seat at the last minute, ditching my bags and running back into the airport right before the plane rolled away from the jet bridge. Okay, well, maybe I was thinking about it a little. But I knew even if Matt asked me to stay one more time, my answer would be the same. New York made sense. The job at Walton made sense. There, I had a concrete future. Here I had nothing but possibilities and questions. "Let's just know that what we have is good." The words were bitter in my mouth.

I kissed Matt fast and with my eyes squeezed shut because I knew if I lingered I could never leave. Then I walked away.

BY the time I pulled my giant suitcase off the baggage claim conveyor belt, it had passed me by three times. I was hollow. My shoulders ached and my head pounded. Having gone through the motions of getting off the plane, turning on my cell phone, texting Elena and my dad, and walking through the sea of disgruntled businesspeople and cheerful families, I had depleted my last stores of energy. Rationally, I knew I couldn't stay at LaGuardia Airport forever. But the idea of sliding into a taxi and sitting on the slick seat protector as the driver navigated to my mother's empty penthouse sent a jolt of pain to my stomach. My phone buzzed in my pocket. Figuring it was Elena, nagging me for the hundredth time to come hang out at her place in the

Village instead of resuming my broodathon, I unlocked the screen without thinking. My heart flipped. Matt.

> *Hey, Mikah. I checked the flight tracker thing and saw you landed. Sorry if that's weird. I should have said this when I dropped you off, but thank you. You made me happy. Wish things could have been different, but I'm real glad we spent the holiday together.*
> *-Matt*

Weirdly it was the fact that Matt actually *signed* his text that had me sagging back against the wall, the force of my sadness crumbling me. It was so… sincere. My fingers were shaking as I tapped the text icon, rereading Matt's words again and again. But I didn't respond. Instead I found a relatively quiet corner, opened Skype, and called the one person who would say the words I needed to hear.

"Mikah?" Her voice was groggy. It was almost midnight in Palermo.

"Nonna…." My throat was so tight, I was surprised I got the word out at all.

"What's wrong?" The sleep was gone from her voice now, and I made out the rustle of sheets and the click of her bedside lamp.

"I made a huge mistake." In a convoluted mess of shaky words and sniffles, I told her the full story of how I met Matt, about how I'd fallen in love with him. I told her about the Walton job and the English opening at the Teton School District. That in the span of six weeks, I had completely rearranged myself. I let all of my fears and hopes and anxieties flow out, and when I stopped talking, I felt better.

My nonna said nothing.

"Like, this is crazy, right? You can't fall in love with someone that fast. It was just a holiday fling. I'm being dramatic, right? And who knows if it would even work—"

"Mikah." She said my name sharply, but not harshly. "This is the man I spoke to on Christmas Eve, yes? The tall, handsome one?"

"Uh-huh."

"The way he looked at you." She sighed into the phone. "He looked at you with love in his eyes. The way your nonno looked at me."

Shit. I didn't want to actually start bawling in the middle of baggage claim, even if it was pretty deserted.

"Do you know how I met your nonno?" she asked, the mischievous edge I knew so well creeping into her tone.

I didn't. I knew almost nothing about my grandfather. He'd been a dockworker. He loved comic books and baking bread. I knew he'd worn the necklace I gave to Matt every day until he died. My face was hot. Would nonna be angry if I told her I'd given my nonboyfriend her late husband's necklace? "No," I said finally.

"You know I loved teaching," she said.

My brows furrowed, confused. I did know this. My nonna's endless supply of stories about her students was part of the reason I'd become a teacher myself.

"But I never told you how hard it was the first week. The kids had no respect. I had no idea what I was doing. It was hard being a working woman in those days. Always when I walked home I cried. One day this big, rough man sat down on the bench next to me. At first he was a little scary. He handed me a handkerchief. His hands were dirty, but the cloth was so clean. I sat down on the bench again the next day. He was there again, this time with a little bag of cookies. We sat on that bench together every day for a whole month and talked. And then he asked me to marry him, and I said yes." I knew she was smiling.

"Seriously? How have I never heard that story? It's, like, rom-com material."

Nonna scoffed. "No. Our love was quiet. But it was easy to love him. When I met him, I knew he was right for me."

"I gave Matt Nonno's necklace for Christmas," I admitted in a rush, all of my breath leaving me.

"Oh, caro, you really love him." Her voice was soft.

"Yeah. I do," I murmured.

"You're strong, Mikah. You will be fine on your own. You know this. But if this man makes you happy, why turn your back on that? Try."

When we ended the call a few minutes later, my body was relaxed, and my mind was clear. If Matt still wanted me, I wanted to try. I hated myself a little at the thought of how much I'd hurt him by walking away from something so good. With Matt, I was a better person. With Matt, my world was a brighter place.

Chapter Fourteen

Matt

THE farm was too quiet. The wind rushed through the open field, rocking my truck and whistling through the spider web of cracks in the passenger side window. It had been ten days since Mikah left.

I'd driven back from the Jackson Hole Airport in silence, knuckles white on the steering wheel. Listening to music felt wrong. Breathing felt wrong. Everything felt wrong. When my front door clicked shut behind me, I'd slumped back against it, sliding down onto the doormat, gripping Mikah's necklace so tight, I thought the small symbol might stay imprinted into my hand forever. Moose laid his head on my lap, and I cried.

He'd texted me once. Two words. *Miss you.* That was it. Even though he'd left, he lingered in my mind's eye: Mikah's face illuminated by firelight on Christmas Eve, the joy in his voice when he told me he loved me, the way he had turned to me in bed on New Year's Eve, deep brown eyes shining. He'd squeezed them shut and a tear trailed down his cheek. I had rubbed it away with my thumb, but more and more followed as I put my arms around him and let him cry.

Now I was hulled out and sick with sadness.

Mikah was bright energy, the glimmer of the sun on the snow. I didn't want to lose him. Part of me wished I'd said aloud what I'd been thinking as I dropped him off at the airport. *Please stay with me. Please let me take care of you. Because I want to be with you. Because being with you is coming home.* The words had expanded, filling my mind, but the thought of saying them felt useless. He'd made his choice, and, even though I didn't understand it, even though it hurt like hell, I had to respect it. One day at a time, I had to get on with my life.

My days were the same as any other winter days on the farm. Get up, work in the greenhouse, tend to the horses, fix what needs fixing. I had gotten used to the empty gut feeling of being lonely. I had gotten used to stretching out alone in my big bed and drinking my coffee in the silent early-morning dark. I had gotten used to rushing through solitary dinners, barely tasting the food I made myself. But being lonely didn't feel normal anymore. I wanted Mikah with me: rolling his pretty brown eyes, waving his hands wildly as he ranted about politics, getting himself worked up and then going all soft and snuggly against me as I kissed him.

Time stretched out, too long and too slow. It was hard to fill my days. My cabin was spotless. I'd tinkered with the tractor so much John told me I was getting close to rebuilding the damn thing. I designed a new logo for the farm. I drove to the library in town and checked out a CD of *The Nutcracker*. Listening to it over and over, I wished I could hear Mikah play the music one more time. Desperate for any distraction, I even paid for expedited shipping on my order of a half-dozen gay cowboy romance novels. I liked them fine, but the happy endings made me weirdly jealous, and I tucked them away on the bottom shelf of my bookcase. A small part of me was bitter, wishing I had never glimpsed the bright satisfaction of loving Mikah. Part of me wished I didn't know what a full, complicated life with someone by my side could look like. But most of me just wanted Mikah to come back.

John and Katie had used the extra cash from the Christmas tree sales to take Abby to an indoor waterpark near Boise she'd been talking about since last summer. So aside from Moose, I really was alone. I knew John felt guilty for going. He could see that I was broken up. He'd even invited me along, saying we could afford to skip a market every now and again. Maybe a change of scenery would do me good. But I'd stayed home, wanting to sleep in my own bed while my sheets still smelled like amber and citrus. I usually washed them every Sunday, but I hadn't been able to. Not while they still smelled like him. Mikah was everywhere. When I rubbed sunscreen onto my face every morning, I thought of the way his eyelashes cast shadows on his smooth, pale skin. When I took down my Christmas tree, I realized Mikah would never see what kind of colorful, glittery ornament Abby put together next year. When I caught a glimpse of the sunset or the stars, I squeezed my eyes shut.

Today had been rough. As I drove to the winter market in Jackson, dread sat heavy in my limbs at the thought that I might see Naomi or Stefano among the crowd of shoppers. As I sold bundles of kale and chatted with market regulars, my mind was a million miles away. Or, really, it was two thousand miles away. I kept trying to picture Mikah in New York, waking up in a tasteful apartment, buying a cup of coffee, his slim body moving through crowded streets I'd never seen before. I couldn't focus. I gave people the wrong change and realized halfway through the market I'd forgotten to bring our entire stock of carrots. I was a total mess.

To make matters worse, it had started snowing hard, big flakes whipping in the wind. The drive back into Idaho from the Teton County Fair Building had been slow and painstaking. Now, as I eased my truck to a stop in front of the barn, I could hardly see two feet in front of me. Moose, who usually dozed in the passenger seat, perked up. He let out a low whine.

The moment I opened my door, my damn dog jumped over me and slipped out of the truck, bolting toward my cabin. It only took a moment for his black shaggy body to disappear into the swirling gusts of snow. What the hell was that about? Moose was a good dog. He never ran off, not even when coyotes or elk drifted out of the forest and into the fields. Quickly, I tossed the bushel baskets and empty coolers in the barn and made sure the horses were set for hay and water. Then I ran after my stupid dog, grumbling the whole way. In all likelihood he would be waiting for me on the porch, soaked but otherwise fine. Tail wagging, eyeing me like, *dude, what took you so long?* The idea of losing him too, of being truly alone, made my stomach clench.

I squinted through the haze of white at a large dark shape outside my cabin. It was too big to be Moose. It was too big to be an *actual* moose. A car? My boots pounded the frozen ground faster. My heart raced. It was the one car I'd desperately hoped to see. Mikah's dented Subaru, covered in a good four inches of snow. Moose was sitting next to the driver's side door like a fluffy, snowy guardian. Then my heart raced for a whole different reason. Was Mikah okay? If he'd seen Moose, I had no doubt he would have let the dog into his car.

When I wiped the glass and bent to look down through the frosted-over window, I grinned, savoring the wave of relief that seeped down to my bones. Mikah sat crumpled in the front seat, wrapped up tight in his black Carhartt coat, fast asleep. His hair was a rumpled mess, and dark circles shaded the thin skin under the spread of his long lashes. His lips were parted and a little swollen, like he'd been biting them nervously. He looked exhausted and so vulnerable. He was the most beautiful thing I'd ever seen. Gently, I knocked on the window.

Mikah started awake, eyes flying open. Through the closed door came a whole lot of mumbling going on as he fumbled with the handle.

"Fuck." The door, which must have been frozen shut, finally gave, and he toppled out of the car, a mess of dark hair, slim limbs, and muttered curses. "Shit. I didn't mean to fall asleep. God, I had this whole big romantic plan. I was just going to, like, show up at your door and kiss you… I mean, only if you wanted that. It kind of occurred to me halfway through my flight that you might not actually want to see me at all again after I was a total asshole and left. And… yeah. Then you weren't home. Obviously. And I guess I fell asleep." His eyebrows crashed together, and he shook his head like he was angry with himself. Moose let out a happy bark at the sight of Mikah. The dog's tail was wagging so fast, it was a black-and-white blur.

I bit the inside of my cheek to keep from laughing. It didn't work. My smile stretched so big, it hurt my face. But I didn't mind. I felt like a little kid, buzzing with the knowledge of his acceptance. His love. "Nice to see you too."

Mikah buried his face in his hands. "Ugh. I seriously am the worst. Matt, I'm so sorry. I shouldn't have left. I don't care about that stupid job. I canceled the interview. I love you and I want to be with you. I *need* to be with you. I want to try, okay?" The words came out fast, muddled together and a little shaky. Mikah paused and swallowed hard, tugging on his hair. He lifted his eyes to meet mine. "Well, uh, I get if you don't want to be with me, though. I acted like an asshole and—"

His words died against my mouth as I pulled him into a tight hug. His warm, soft lips and tiny sigh were everything I'd missed as I lay awake every night, staring at the ceiling in the cold solitude of my cabin. He collapsed against me with a soft whimper. Then Mikah's thin arms twined around my neck, and I could feel him smiling. I lifted him against me, and he wrapped his legs around my waist. We kissed and kissed until my hair was soaked with snow, and I could feel Mikah shivering in my arms. I set him down gently but kept holding him close. He nuzzled into my chest. The snow had drifted around us, piling up over the tops of my work boots. I was getting cold. But I didn't want to stop holding him. Ever.

As much as I loved the sweetness of Mikah's lips and I really couldn't wait to take him to bed, it was the perfect weight of him in my arms I'd missed the most. Until I met him, I'd never exactly held anyone. One-armed bro hugs with John. Quick hugs with Katie and Abby. My parents weren't huggers. But hauling Mikah in close against me, wrapping him up in my arms, feeling his chest rise and fall in time with mine, was undeniably right. I felt not just needed but wanted. Like this was where he was meant to be. Where I was meant to be. I pressed my lips to the top of his head and breathed his smell. "Baby, you know I want you here. Always. I love you so much." I had to clear my throat.

Mikah's eyes locked on mine, the deep brown burning with need and love and possibility. "I know you do," he murmured. He cupped my face with one cold hand, his slim fingers rubbing over my jaw, my cheeks, the cold exposed skin on the back of my neck. He pulled me down to him.

Our lips were only inches apart when Moose snuffled at Mikah's black boots and whined. Clearly the dog was feeling starved for attention. "I think he missed you as much as I did." I laughed.

Mikah grinned down at Moose, squatting to ruffle the frosty fur on top of the dog's head. Moose leaned so heavily against his delicate frame that he almost tipped over into the snow. Mikah shot to his feet. "Oh, no. Not today, dog. I am *not* ruining this moment even more by getting knocked on my ass. Not happening."

"Well, if you want, you can come inside and defrost. You can even borrow my clothes again. Might even make you hot chocolate." I smirked. Damn, if I'd known selling Christmas trees was going to bring the love of my life right to my door, I might have been a hell of a lot more enthusiastic about the idea when John first brought it up.

"Oh, thank God. It's freezing out here." Mikah's smile was pure joy.

I took his hand in mine and kissed him as the snow swirled around us. Then, together, we made our way inside, where I knew everything would be warm and bright.

Epilogue

The Following Christmas Eve
Matt

"SHIT!" Mikah's eyes went wide and frantic as he slid his hand between the couch cushions. There was a smear of flour on the sharp line of his cheekbone, and his black jeans were dotted with white handprints. He tugged hard at the neck of his loosely knit dark-gray sweater, a sure sign he was getting stressed. Now I knew why all of his sweaters and T-shirts were in such rough shape. "I can't find it anywhere." He shot me a pleading expression.

"This?" I held up his cell phone, which I found right where he left it, on the kitchen counter surrounded by a mess of recipe cards. I tried to hide my smirk but knew I'd failed when Mikah rolled his eyes.

"Oh, don't be so proud of yourself." He snapped the phone out of my hand. But almost immediately his expression relaxed, and his cheeks flushed an adorable shade of pink. "Sorry. Thank you. I really want everything to be right," he murmured, pushing up onto the balls of his feet to brush his lips over mine. He tasted like orange and vanilla. I moaned into the heat of his mouth, my skin tingling with arousal. Even after a year together, everything about Mikah turned me on so fast, it was almost embarrassing. I couldn't help but deepen the kiss, sliding my hands down to his slim hips and tugging him close. He gasped and licked into me, going pliant against my body for just a moment. "No! I don't have time for this. Stop distracting me." He grinned and swatted my ass before darting back to the kitchen, cell phone in hand.

I tried not to pout. "Baby, it doesn't have to be perfect," I reminded him for what felt like the hundredth time. "And you can let me help you, you know."

"You already did the cookies. And these need to come out of the oven…." He glanced at the clock and scrambled for the oven mitts. "Three minutes ago. Fuck."

Of course when he slid the panettone out of the oven and did some complicated inversion involving string and a cooling rack so the Christmas breads could cool upside down, they were perfect, golden-brown domes. The whole cabin smelled like citrus and warm butter with the ever-present resin undercurrent of pine. Moose snoozed by the fire, his big white belly rising and falling with his loud snores. Outside it was snowing, light flakes drifting slowly toward the already thick blanket of powder that had fallen overnight.

I smiled to myself at how much my house—hell, my whole existence—had changed since Moose knocked Mikah into the snow the year before. My cabin was no longer a meticulously tidy, lonely place. Mikah made sure of that. In August, after weeks of a simmering argument that had finally boiled over into our first actual fight, I'd finally convinced him to move out of the tiny studio he'd been renting in town and into my cabin full-time. When Mikah blew back into my life that January afternoon, we'd spent the first few days after his arrival holed up in bed. Then we'd spent the next few talking so much I'd been pretty sure I had used up my lifetime supply of words. I'd listened while Mikah panicked over applying for the job at Teton High School. He'd held my hand in his and murmured reassuring words as I admitted I was worried he might leave again. And we'd talked together for a long time about what we wanted an actual relationship to look like. Twined together in bed, we'd whispered into the dark the things we wanted for the future: adopting another dog, traveling to Italy, maybe even having a family someday. But Mikah explained that he wasn't quite ready to live with me full-time yet, so he'd found a place to rent in Driggs. At first, I'd totally understood his need for space and his desire to take things slow. But by the time summer rolled around, he'd been spending so much time at my place anyway it seemed ridiculous for him to pay the rent on that dump of an apartment.

When he'd finally decided he was ready to move in, Mikah brought so many books, I'd only been half joking when I grumbled about having to build a whole second house to hold all of them. Now, though, the poetry books and classics and the surprisingly large collection of romance novels I'd built up over time were neatly arranged on the simple pine bookshelves I built to accommodate them. Most of the time, the kitchen counter was a mess of essays and worksheets that Mikah claimed were organized in a specific "system" but mostly seemed like an explosion of haphazard binder-clipped piles. He was forever leaving his shoes in the middle of the rug and abandoning half-full coffee cups on top of the dresser. He never hung his coat on the hook, always throwing it over the back of his favorite armchair. He had stuffed the bathroom medicine cabinet with so many face serums, moisturizers, and clay masks that I grimaced every time I opened the thing, thinking one of the expensive vials was going to crash to the tile floor. So I'd built a small shelf for the bathroom too.

I loved it. For the first time in the ten years since I'd built the place, the cabin felt lived in. Like home. Big abstract paintings by New York City artists Mikah's mom knew hung on the walls alongside Abby's portrait of Moose and a painting she'd done of Mikah and me for my birthday. I'd actually laughed out loud when I unwrapped it. As much as that kid loved making everything as colorful as possible, she'd been true to life, using only shades of black, white, brown, and gray to paint my boyfriend.

Mikah's phone buzzed on the counter, and he scrambled to unlock the screen, almost dropping it in the process. "Oh God," he yelped, "they're on their way already. Shit." His eyes darted from the Christmas tree, a big spruce we cut down together and decked out in colorful lights and the usual mess of Abby-made ornaments, to the arrangement of daisies, white roses, and pine springs I had set on the coffee table.

I knew he was nervous about his nonna and mom, who had both arrived the day before, seeing our place for the first time. To ease his mind, I had spent the morning making sure everything was spotless and cheerfully decorated. I'd even driven to the flower shop in Jackson that Naomi recommended instead of picking up a bouquet from the supermarket. The place looked as nice as it possibly could. And really, I was the one who should be nervous. I'd skyped with Mikah's nonna a handful of times and had spoken on the phone with Mikah's mom, or Luciana as she'd insisted I call her, on a few occasions too. But meeting them in person was different. Especially tonight. Blood rushed in my ears, and my hand went instinctively to my chest, squeezing quick and tight around the necklace. I was definitely the one who should be nervous.

Wrapping my arms around Mikah from behind, I held him tight against me, my face buried in his hair, until I felt him relax. Then I turned him around. "Sweetheart, you need to calm down." I kissed his forehead and his eyes fluttered closed.

"I know. I know." He sighed heavily. "They're only going to be here for, like, five minutes anyway. I just want them to... get it, I guess. I want them to understand how happy I am or whatever. I'm pretty sure my mom thought I, like, had a mental breakdown when I decided to move out here. She would one hundred percent not know what to do with herself without delivery sushi. Starve, I guess." Mikah's smile was tense, defensive. His armor smile. I smoothed it away with my thumb, and a real grin replaced it.

At first, Mikah had wanted to host Christmas Eve dinner at our place, planning to cook the whole seafood meal himself for everyone in our tiny kitchen. He had not been happy when I pointed out that our two-seat breakfast bar wouldn't exactly be the best place to serve a meal for a dozen people. Even if I moved all of the furniture out of the living room and into the barn, and even if we ate picnic-style on the floor, it would be cramped in our small cabin. And although I had big plans for adding on two bedrooms, an eating area, and a big patio, those would have to wait until I had a slightly clearer view of our future. Until after tonight.

"It'll be all right." I ruffled Mikah's hair, and he scoffed, running his fingers through it to smooth the dark curls. "John and Katie have everything ready at their place. I talked to John, like, twenty minutes ago, okay? Everything is going to be fine." I needed to convince myself of that too.

Mikah nodded but still looked worried, chewing on his lower lip. I knew he wasn't happy about giving up control of the Christmas Eve dinner. Katie, wanting to be helpful, had offered to host everyone at their place. That also meant she would be doing the cooking, putting her own spin on the Italian meal. Mikah had agreed enthusiastically, but I suspected that the idea of a Christmas Eve without the baccalà and seafood salad was actually killing him.

At the sound of several car doors slamming outside, Mikah's frantic energy reached levels I'd only seen after he interviewed for the teaching job at Teton High. His poor sweater would probably never recover. Moose, seeming to sense Mikah's distress, and maybe a little of mine, hauled himself up from his post by the woodstove and butted Mikah's hand with his snout. Glancing out the front windows, I saw Stefano's gleaming black Mercedes and a white Audi SUV. Luca was leaning against his dad's car, phone in hand. Elena caught my eye through the window and waved excitedly, her face almost completely hidden behind a huge red scarf. Next to her, a striking person with dark buzzed hair gazed calmly at the snow-

cloaked landscape, seeming unperturbed by the gusts
of icy wind. Stefano and Naomi both carried tote bags
that I knew would be stuffed full of cookies, wine, and
tasteful presents. Mikah's nonna climbed out of the car,
followed quickly by his mother. I swallowed hard.

"Mikah, this place is stunning. So simple."
Mikah's mother pulled her son into what seemed to
be a bone-crushing hug the moment he opened the
door. Neither of them seemed to notice that they were
blocking everyone else from coming inside. She let him
go, still grasping his shoulders, then turned to look at
me. I had been right when I'd guessed that Mikah and
Elena took after their mom. But where Mikah and his
sister were delicate and a little messy, she was intense
and very polished. She was beautiful and petite, with
glossy dark hair tumbling down her back and flawless
makeup. Her deep red velvet coat, embroidered with an
elaborate pattern of gold flowers, definitely looked like
the kind of thing I should hang up in the closet, instead
of flopping it on our bed with everyone else's. "Matt,"
she said in an accent that reminded me of old movies,
all smooth and sophisticated, "*piacere*. It is lovely to
meet you in person. My God—" She kissed my cheeks
quickly before turning to Mikah. "—well done, caro.
Che bello!"

The back of my neck got hot, and I rubbed at it.
"Nice to meet you, ma'am."

"Luciana, please." She patted my face.

"Mamma, keep moving. We're freezing out here,"
Elena's voice called from the porch.

Then the cabin was bursting with motion: fierce
hugs, fast kisses, shrugging out of coats, Moose
desperately trying to greet everyone at once. I hung back.
Mikah's grandmother grabbed his hand, the two of them

immediately falling into what sounded like a heated conversation in Italian, their voices rising and gestures growing in size as they drifted into the living room. She was about Mikah's height, with a long silver braid, dressed in loose-fitting black pants and a floral blouse. Although she and Mikah glanced over at me a few times as they spoke, she clearly only had eyes for her grandson. I grinned, looking at the fire for a long moment. It was nice to know someone loved Mikah as much as I did.

"Okay, people. Introductions." Elena clapped her hands together, two clipped, sharp sounds. I was only a little surprised when everyone fell silent. She shot me a wicked grin. "This is Matt, my brother's supersexy farmer boyfriend who makes him insanely happy. He's kind of shy, but he's the sweetest."

My ears throbbed and my scalp tingled. I lifted my hand in a silent greeting toward Mikah's nonna and the person next to Elena. From across the room where he stood arm-in-arm with his grandmother, Mikah blew me a kiss. I relaxed a little.

"Sorry, Matt." Elena winked at me dramatically, then turned to the person standing so close to her, the two seemed to be a mass of loose, flowing neutral clothing. "This is my partner, Jo. Just a quick pronoun thing, Jo uses they or them. Cool?" She nodded definitively at Mikah, who was looking between his sister and Jo with a fond, soft expression. Jo glanced at me, their expression a little wary. I inclined my head and smiled, hoping I seemed welcoming and not at all intimidating. "Great." Elena gave Jo a quick kiss on the cheek. "Well, obviously the rest of us know each other so…."

"Okay, then, weirdo." Mikah shook his head at his sister. "We have wine if anyone wants some, and Matt made some spiced cider." I hurried to follow him into the kitchen, needing something to do with my hands. But soft fingers wrapped around my wrist, stopping me before I could help out with getting drinks.

"It looks good on you." Mikah's nonna patted my chest where the Trinacria necklace rested on top of the denim shirt Mikah had insisted was fancy enough for the evening.

"Thanks." I had gone over all of the things I wanted to say to her in my head: thanking her for pushing Mikah to come back to me, telling her how much I loved her grandson, maybe even bringing up the question that had been turning itself over endlessly in my mind for the last few months. But my brain suddenly felt sluggish, and I couldn't seem to make my mouth move.

She looked at me for a long moment; then a slow, soft smile spread over her face, like she somehow read my mind. "Thank you," she spoke quietly, "for making my Mikah so happy."

I swear my heart stopped. Slipping my hand into my pocket, I closed my fingers around the small pouch I'd tucked there while Mikah was swearing over the panettone dough.

Mikah

MATT was acting weird. Of course I knew he was nervous to actually meet my mom and nonna in person. And I knew he didn't love crowds. But as he'd helped me pack up the panettone and gather up the gifts to bring over to John and Katie's, he'd been almost stonily silent, not meeting my eye. And now as we all stomped through the knee-deep snow, shivering and chatting,

Matt walked by himself with his hands shoved deep into the pockets of his coat. Moose bounded behind him, popping up and down in the snow like a dolphin in water. It was already getting dark, and I looked up at the sky, the misty pink behind the mountains fading to deep purple. I tried to get Matt's attention, since we usually made it a point to watch the sunset together, but his gaze was fixed firmly to the frozen earth. I tugged my coat tight around me against the chill.

"Merry Christmas, everybody!" Katie called from the open front door, soft yellow light spilling onto the freshly fallen snow. She'd gone all out on the decorations this year: outlining the house's trim in colored lights, bordering the walkway with sparkly candy canes, and dotting the front yard with illuminated white wicker deer even though the real-life versions were in no short supply. Abby appeared at Katie's side, seeming a little shy as a huge throng of mostly strange people descended on her home. The two of them wore matching Christmas sweaters, bright green with a subtle pine tree pattern. Matt had told me about John's collection of garish holiday sweaters, and I couldn't wait to see what Katie's mother had knitted for him this year.

I hurried through the introductions again as we shed our coats and winter boots in the entryway. The sound of *Elf,* Abby's absolute favorite Christmas movie, filtered in from the den. She had made Matt and I watch it at least ten times over the last few weeks. The smell of Katie's house surrounded me, a comforting mix of cinnamon candles and the familiar whisper of the rose perfume she always wore. The air was also heavy with the scent of garlic and oregano, and I grinned at how seriously she'd committed to the task of preparing an Italian Christmas meal.

Getting to know Katie had been an unexpected bright spot in my radically transformed new life in the Teton Valley. She was fierce and wonderful. After helping me through the process of transferring my teaching certification to Idaho, I had a strong suspicion that she'd pulled some strings to guarantee I got the job teaching ninth-grade English at Teton High School. And once the school year had started, she'd proven herself to be an amazing coworker and a strong ally. Although I had no interest in being closeted at work, I'd been a little anxious about how teachers and students, not to mention parents, would feel about this new gay outsider at their school. Katie had encouraged me to simply mention my leadership role with my last school's gay-straight alliance in my introductory letter to families at the outset of the year. For the most part, my sexuality was a nonissue. When one parent caused a small fuss about the school hiring a gay teacher, Katie helped me start a brand-new LGBTQ club. I was certain that the transition to rural life would not have been as easy without Katie's endless supply of positivity and pragmatism.

Although John and Katie's kitchen wasn't very big, we all ended up gravitating to the space, with the exception of Luca and John, who made a hasty retreat to the garage. My mom and Naomi were chatting pleasantly about some juice cleanse they'd both done, while Abby asked my nonna dozens of questions about Italy. Jo and Elena were embroiled in a political debate with my father. Thankfully, though, no one seemed to have gotten aggravated yet. And Matt stood with his back against the refrigerator, his jaw tight, staring fixedly at the Christmas tree in the living room. What was going on with him?

"Baby, are you okay?" I crossed the kitchen and stepped between his feet.

Matt jerked, like he'd been so zoned out, he forgot we were all there. "Yup. Fine. Sorry."

I wrinkled my eyebrows and looked at him closely. Matt's tendency to go taciturn when something was bothering him was something we were working on. He kept a lot inside, whereas I needed to talk through every little issue for hours on end. I had never seen him so visibly tense. Did he not like my mom? She could be kind of a big personality. Maybe she'd said something weird to him. "Are you sure?" Grabbing his shoulders, I kissed the tip of his nose.

He smirked. "I'm fine. Really. Just hungry."

I turned to Katie, who was pulling what looked like a third pan of lasagna out of the oven. The concrete countertop was lined with pan after foil-covered pan of stuffed shells, baked ziti, lasagna, and something she'd called meatball casserole. I couldn't wait to see the look on Luca's face when we sat down to eat. He was notoriously pretentious about food, once mentioning offhandedly he didn't go to restaurants in LA that "most people" could get into. Whatever the hell that meant.

Fortunately, Luca was polite as we all crowded into mismatched chairs around John and Katie's gigantic dining table. Katie, of course, had gone all out on the decorations here too. The table was draped with a red-and-green plaid tablecloth and adorned with glass jars of glittery ornaments. The dinner plates were Christmas-themed too, depicting snowmen engaged in a variety of cheerful winter pursuits. I smiled at the memory of building a snowman with Abby and John last week, once my Christmas break had started and I'd needed a break from grading the mountain of creative essays on *The House on Mango Street* that I deeply regretted assigning. Abby had, naturally, decided that the snowman would look better if we decorated it with rocks, and the final result had, honestly, looked pretty terrifying. When Matt got back from the market and saw the thing, he had actually seemed a little freaked-out by it.

I helped Katie fill wineglasses and pour water while everyone else served themselves buffet-style in the kitchen.

"Why is Matt acting so weird?" I whispered to Katie, casting a quick glance at my boyfriend's broad retreating back.

She bit her lip and shrugged but wouldn't meet my eye. "He seems fine to me."

"He so does not. I mean I know he's not, like, Mr. Talkative or anything. But he's barely said two words since my family got here. I was really excited for him to meet my nonna. But he's being kind of unfriendly, don't you think?"

Katie's mouth twitched, and she started aggressively smoothing the already perfectly smooth tablecloth. Okay, so now she was acting weird too. "Mikah, he's just—" She paused. "I wouldn't worry about it, all right?" Her voice simmered with suppressed mirth.

Holy fucking shit. There was no way. Was Matt going to propose to me on Christmas Eve? *This* Christmas Eve? Tonight? My brain kicked into overdrive, exploring the possibility, then quickly shutting it down in an endless loop, until Matt came back into the dining room with two plates of food. One was heaped with meatballs, garlic bread, and at least four kinds of pasta. The other bore one small slice of lasagna and a big pile of salad. Matt had finally learned that not everyone ate enormous portions like he did. Then again, not everyone spent their waking hours hauling heavy things around and working the land.

I couldn't stop my knee from bouncing as I slid into my chair next to Matt. I took a big gulp of wine and looked around the table. Did everyone else know? John, who was indeed wearing a truly awful Christmas sweater with three gingerbread men in the middle of his chest, was already wolfing down his food. Luca was sipping the wine with a dubious expression on his face. Elena and Jo were still arguing politics with my dad, and Abby seemed to have found a new favorite person in my nonna. I caught my grandmother's eye and flicked my gaze to Matt. She smiled serenely and returned her attention to Abby.

Once everyone was settled with their food, my dad lightly tapped his wineglass with his knife and gave a brief toast. Thankfully, he stuck exclusively to English as he spoke about our families coming together and the beauty of love. I tried not to get weepy. Then John stood, and in a thick, gruff voice, thanked everyone for coming. He fixed me with a long look as he thanked me for making his little brother the second happiest man in the world. Matt put his hand over mine on the table, and I buried my face in his shoulder. I could have stayed like that all night, my cheek pressed against the rough denim of his shirt, breathing his smell, like comfort and home. But my brother's voice made me sit up straight.

"Mikah, I don't want to put a damper on the evening or anything, but I do want to take a quick second to apologize to you. And to Matt." Both of our faces must have registered confusion because Luca looked between us and laughed. He sounded kind of nervous. "Honestly, when you moved out here, I thought you'd lost it, bro. I figured this whole thing was destined to crash and burn and we'd have to help you get your shi—um, stuff together all over again."

I gaped at my brother. *Wow, Luca, tell me what you really think.* Matt squeezed my hand and smirked at me.

"But seeing you guys together, it's clear that this works. So I'm sorry for always being so overprotective and for not trusting you. You guys basically made my jaded ass believe in love. So, Merry Christmas." He scrubbed a hand over his face and sat back down, looking uncharacteristically embarrassed.

"Such a nice speech, Luca." Elena's voice dripped with sarcasm as she shook her head fondly.

"And don't cuss in front of my kid." Katie winked, but Luca looked even more uncomfortable.

As everyone settled back into eating and chatting, I wanted to crawl out of my skin. The meal was a blur of conversations I couldn't follow and hyperawareness of the man next to me. Anytime Matt shifted in his seat, my heart leapt to my throat and I was convinced he was about to get down on one knee. While I was sure the lasagna was delicious, I barely registered the taste. By the time I robotically stood to help Katie and John clear the plates, I'd about worn myself out.

"Mikah, don't you dare start on those dishes. Let's leave 'em for later," Katie said as I followed her into the kitchen. "Cut up your fruit bread and make some coffee. Then I want you to sit and relax. Just lookin' at you is stressing me out."

Once everyone was settled in the den, sipping coffee and enjoying dessert, I relaxed. Clearly, I had been wrong about the Christmas proposal thing. Honestly, although we had talked about getting engaged, I doubted Matt would be comfortable doing something so personal in front of an audience. Maybe he was tense about being around so many people. He seemed pretty relaxed now, though, his arm slung easily around me. John had turned on an Elvis Christmas album, the rich, smooth voice achingly familiar. Aside from the low music, the living room was quiet. Everyone was sleepy and satisfied. Abby sat at the base of the Christmas tree, gazing up at the twinkly lights and mismatched ornaments. I snuggled into Matt's side where we sat on the floor in front of the woodstove. Bathed in the wash of pinkish-gold firelight, everything was soft and perfect. Like a good dream. I grinned to myself, remembering how I'd assumed nothing would be better than last Christmas with Matt. How I'd been so sure I would look back on that night and feel nothing but sweet sorrow. Now, the memories of playing the piano for him, exchanging gifts in front of the fire, snuggling on our couch filled me with so much joy I almost couldn't contain it.

In all of my worrying and second-guessing over what would ultimately bring me happiness, I never would have guessed that I could find such profound joy in the simple, quotidian details. But it was the small things with Matt that made life feel easy and safe. The way Matt, always rising before the sun, moved through the cabin in the dark to make coffee and bring it to me in bed. The way he always pressed a kiss to my hair before heading out to the field. The way I'd complained once about the cafeteria food at school and the next morning I found a bagged lunch waiting for me in the fridge. The way we just fit. I trusted Matt, trusted our life together.

The brush of Matt's lips on my temple startled me from my drowsy, contented thoughts. I was burrowed into his warmth, eyelids heavy. Shit, had I been falling asleep? And why was everyone staring at me?

"Mikah?" Matt's lips quirked up. "You awake, baby?"

"Oh, sorry. Yeah. I was um…. Sorry. What's up?" I rubbed my eyes.

Matt grabbed the back of his neck and looked at me for a long moment. Then he rose to his feet in a smooth motion, fumbling around in his pocket. My stomach flipped. His blue eyes were still locked on my face as he sank down to one knee, his gaze once again level with mine. Holy shit.

"Are you proposing to me right now?" My voice was high with incredulity. All of the breath seemed to have rushed out of my body.

"Um, yup." His hands, so big and rugged, came to rest on my shoulders.

I swallowed hard and tried to etch every detail of the moment in my brain: the tiny cut on Matt's chin where he'd nicked himself shaving this morning, the silver wash of moonlight on the snow outside—the way Matt was looking at me like I was everything he wanted. "Well, go ahead, then...."

He shook his head and scrubbed a hand over his face, clearly amused and a little flustered. His cheeks and ears flushed pink. "You know what I want to ask you."

"Dude, you have to actually say it," John supplied from his spot in the armchair.

I laughed shakily, but my eyes filled with tears, blurring Matt's face and the glow of the Christmas tree behind it. Happiness burned bright inside me.

"Okay, okay," Matt grumbled, "Mikah, I love you. You make me happier than I ever hoped I would be. I never thought I would find someone who makes my life so... good. And I want us to spend the rest of it together." His voice dropped low, and he cleared his throat. There were tears in his eyes too. "Do you want to get married?"

I nodded convulsively, but no words would come. Matt opened his palm, revealing two simple gold wedding bands. Clearly he'd been holding them tight. His rough hand showed small circular indentations where he'd been gripping the rings. They were perfect. He was perfect. I tipped forward so fast my head spun a little, and pressed my lips to his, savoring his steadfast heat. "I love you so much," I breathed into the tiny sliver of air between our faces. "And, of course, I really fucking want to marry you."

Although I'd barely whispered the words, everyone in the living room erupted into cheers of congratulations. Distantly, I was aware of our families: the pop of a champagne cork, Katie muttering about how we all swore like sailors, a swirl of excited chatter about when and where we would have the wedding. Matt rose to stand, bringing me up with him and drawing me in close. I was exactly where I wanted to be, safe and warm in the arms of the man I loved. I was home. And I could stay there forever.

Coming Soon

⊚ REAMSPUN DESIRES

Santa's Last Gift by Sandine Tomas

The greatest gift might be what they already have.

After years away building his career, event planner Sebastian Chesnut returns to his small hometown of Fir Falls to reconnect with his mother, sister, and young nieces before his job takes him to London.

He doesn't expect to find his high school boyfriend, Matty, has become a virtual member of Seb's family. Back then, Matty only offered a casual relationship, but Seb fell hard, and history is soon repeating itself. Seb's afraid to hope for a second chance, no matter how much they've grown and despite the family they share. Instead, he focuses on creating a last perfect holiday, which won't be easy with his sister's ex planning to take the girls over Christmas.

Seb and Matty might not know what to do about their feelings for each other, but one thing's for sure—it won't be Christmas without the kids. Can these star-crossed lovers pull off a holiday miracle?

Silent Heart by Amy Lane

Dog wrangler Preston Echo has been in love with his brother's best friend, copilot, and business partner since high school—and Damien Ward knew it. As Preston grew into a stunning, hard-willed man, Damien began to dream of Preston too.

Then Damien almost died in a helicopter crash. While his physical wounds are slowly healing, the blows to his self-confidence and goodwill are almost worse. His body is broken and he's afraid to fly—how can Preston love him now?

When Preston's brother goes on a search-and-rescue mission and disappears in an earthquake zone in Mexico, Preston and Damien are thrown together in an effort to find him and bring him back. Preston's merciless honesty—and relentless passion—may leverage Damien into his bed, but can Damien overcome his fears to allow himself to stay there?